TWISTED TALES

FIENDISH STORIES

Edited By Sarah Waterhouse

First published in Great Britain in 2022 by:

 Young**Writers**® ━ Est. 1991 ━

Young Writers
Remus House
Coltsfoot Drive
Peterborough
PE2 9BF
Telephone: 01733 890066
Website: www.youngwriters.co.uk

Printed and bound in the UK by BookPrintingUK
Website: www.bookprintinguk.com
YB0500M

FOREWORD

Welcome, Reader!

Come into our lair, there's really nothing to fear. You may have heard bad things about the villains within these pages, but there's more to their stories than you might think...

For our latest competition, Twisted Tales, we challenged secondary school students to write a story in just 100 words that shows us another side to the traditional storybook villain. We asked them to look beyond the evil escapades and tell a story that shows a bad guy or girl in a new light. They were given optional story starters for a spark of inspiration, and could focus on their motivation, back story, or even what they get up to in their downtime!

And that's exactly what the authors in this anthology have done, giving us some unique new insights into those we usually consider the villain of the piece. The result is a thrilling and absorbing collection of stories written in a variety of styles, and it's a testament to the creativity of these young authors.

Here at Young Writers it's our aim to inspire the next generation and instill in them a love of creative writing, and what better way than to see their work in print? The imagination and skill within these pages are proof that we might just be achieving that aim! Congratulations to each of these fantastic authors.

CONTENTS

Georgina Cormican (12) 63
Faith Sole (12) & Calum 64
Zach Moorman (14) 65
Jorge Mullan-Starr (14) 66
Luca Costello (12) 67
Michelle Kelly (14) 68
Chelsy Rainey (14) 69
Josh Megarry-Hewitt (13) 70
Freya Mullen (13) 71
Mason Lovell (13) 72
Brooke Gilmore (12) 73
Olivia Belmar (11) 74
Lucie Watson (11) 75
Katy-Mae Hopkins (14) 76
Katie-Rose Wallace (12) 77
Nathan Belmar (12) 78
Lorenzo Lauro (11) 79
Declan Duvey (11) 80
Scott Boston (13) 81
Geordan Mullen (14) 82
Holly Knox (14) 83

Great Yarmouth Charter Academy, Great Yarmouth

Phoebie Allen (12) 84
Beth Noble (14) 85
Iris Vaz (13) 86
Kaiden Carapinha (12) 87
Cristina Gabrieli (13) 88
Paris Jonas-Smith (11) 89
Rumer Skidmore (13) 90
Isobel Tann (12) 91
Emilee Sweeney (12) 92
Kelsie Stringer (14) 93
Emma Lilley (14) 94
Eda Revuckaite (13) 95
Rachael Bailey (13) 96
Patricia Staff (11) 97
Ella Ellis (13) 98
Daisy Hills (11) 99
Marcio Rocha (14) 100
Imogen Butcher (12) 101
Mason Pitts-Cross (12) 102

Phoebe Carter (13) 103
Scarlett Hudson (11) 104
Yasmina Rosu (11) 105
Frejya McCluskey (11) 106
Angel Wilkin (12) 107
Gerda Skiragyte (11) 108
Thomas Malins (14) 109
Alyssa Basset-Oldfield (13) 110
Chloe Ashworth (15) 111
Rhys Saiche (16) 112

St Ives School, Higher Tregenna

Megan Harvey (13) 113
Evie Oatham (14) 114
Gwen Fryer (11) 115
Leo Kirk-Mackrell (12) 116
Rowan Kemp (12) 117
Freya-Lilly Powell (12) 118
Solomon Richards (12) 119
Alfie Smith (11) 120
Yves Armstrong-Donaldson (12) 121
Gracie Dorrell (13) 122
Maggie Mansell (12) 123
Tyler Barrett (12) 124
Harvey Williams (13) 125
Fearne Slade (14) 126
Kai Austin (12) 127
Chloe Wills (12) 128
Danielle Fox (14) 129
Katie Cook (12) 130
Etienne Fulker (11) 131
Phoebe Bradbury (12) 132
Rupert Bell (13) 133
Olive A-Chapman (13) 134
Ysella Thomas (12) 135
Laurence Wallis (12) 136
Martin Wright (12) 137
Edie Price (12) 138
Will Bramwell (13) 139
Freya Scorer (13) 140
Toby Wilkinson (12) 141
Ashley Davies (14) 142
Brooke Bonner (12) 143

Kiki Fox (11)	144	Shahmeer Khattak (13)	184
Andy Sully (12)	145		
Lily Ferris (13)	146		
Mason Aldrich (13)	147		
Lucie Cole (12)	148		
Maddison Franklin (12)	149		
Elliot Symons (13)	150		
Isla Thornton (12)	151		
Caleb Woodcroft (13)	152		
Isaac Walsh (12)	153		
Ethan Quinn (14)	154		
Rocky Palmer (12)	155		
Camilla Bennie Louise (12)	156		
Willow Tarplee (12)	157		
Dylan Kemp (13)	158		
Teddy Nichols (13)	159		
Harriet Hartley (12)	160		
Archie Cooper (12)	161		
Ophelia Musto Shinton (11)	162		
Gabriel Musto-Shinton (13)	163		
Will Clayton (12)	164		
Rune Gustafsson (11)	165		
Poppy Taylor (12)	166		
Amiee Simpson (11)	167		
Ollie Herbert (11)	168		
Eachan Wilson (12)	169		
Catrin Berriman (12)	170		
Perran Metcalfe-Waller (13)	171		
Oscar Wills (12)	172		
N J Nicholls (12)	173		
Jack Thomas (12)	174		
Senara Beeson (13)	175		

Walton High Brooklands Campus, Brooklands

Archie Morton (13)	176
Zebbi Dixon-Osei (14)	177
Sophia Patsavellas (14)	178
Skye Welsh (14)	179
Luther Brown	180
Disha Kharod (14)	181
Aaliyah Salum (13)	182
Calum Pickett (13)	183

THE
STORIES

THE BEAUTY PAGEANT

"Come on, you're not going to be Queen Grimhide if you don't look prettier."

"Ow, ow! You're hurting me!"

"I don't care that you are hurting, you will look prettier."

"I think you have broken my ribs!"

"So what? Remind me, what's your show name?"

"The Evil Queen."

"Right, showtime. Go on, move, get on the stage!"

"Now coming on stage, the Evil Queen."

I hated that day. I broke two ribs and didn't win, so my mum told me, "You are not pretty enough," and she left me. That's why I am so obsessed with me looking good.

Iona McFadzean (12)

Alness Academy, Alness

TWISTED TALES

A while back, the nicest student in Dreemurr School became friends with the bully.
Earlier today, they went to the library and disappeared.
"Hey Kris, where the heck are we?" asked Suzie (the bully).
"Well, Kris, I guess we have to split up now," sighed Suzie.
"Okay, I'll meet up with you later," replied Kris. Kris met up with Noelle, the second-best student. They walked along, freezing everything in the dark world until they saw the third best student. Berdly ran and attacked Kris and Noelle, but they defended themselves and Kris demanded Noelle use Snowgrave to kill Berdly...

Seth Calder (12)
Alness Academy, Alness

TWISTED TALES

"Did you get that, lads?

"Yes!" they all said as we set sail in our pirate ship. We couldn't wait to steal our treasure back that Redbeard stole. When we got on the roaring rocky river, everything went downhill. We were going left and right, trying to dodge the huge rocks, and when we made it out, everyone got seasick. "That was a thrilling ride," said one of the crew members.

"It will get even more thrilling from here!" I shouted. When we arrived on the island, we went looking for the Redbeard. But he stole our ship and escaped.

Nafih Karuthedath (13)

Alness Academy, Alness

PORTRAYAL

I can't believe it. I'm in the dark dimension where almost everything's the same, but without humanity. Everything that happens, happens here too, but without humanity, it's all falling apart. I heard a scream and a sound that sounded like two bones cracking together and a heart pumping in my ear. Silence... Two bony hands gripped around my ankles. "Help me!" I heard from below and I almost collapsed after I looked. It was me, but different. They looked starved. They grabbed my hand tightly, I pulled him up, then saw his eyes and he twisted me to the edge...

William Milne (14)
Alness Academy, Alness

THE LITTLE MERMAID

Ariel, voiceless on the third night, was trying to get a true love's kiss from the prince, but Ursula was taking her place. His lips touched hers. Then Ariel realised the sun had gone down. Ursula turned back into herself. She grabbed hold of Ariel, not letting go. She couldn't scream. Underwater, Ursula pulled her down deeper until Ariel couldn't breathe. The prince went after them. He went deeper and deeper, but he had to go back for air. Ariel's father was going after Ursula, but she was too quick with her long tentacles. Ursula had a good feast tonight.

Chloe Fraser (12)
Alness Academy, Alness

PRESSURED

Helplessly running through fields, trying to get away from these intrusive thoughts, screaming but no one can hear me, something's pulling me back. Won't let me go. I can feel them, but no one's really there. I can hear heavy panting in my ears. Everywhere I turn, someone's at the end but disappearing from my eyes, grabbing my hair, screaming for help. It's only me here. I fall to the ground. Feels like sinking. I can't breathe. Someone's holding me, cutting my breath. I see them over me. These thoughts have grown into a man. He's now my villain.

Summer Gemmell Alexander (13)
Alness Academy, Alness

YOU

This is your story, nobody else's, yours. Nobody will take credit for your work; there isn't anyone who can take credit for your work. All your achievements in one place. And they're not just for you! Anyone can read this, so that means you can make yourself look however you want, right? Well, it's not always that simple. Sure, anything you want you can write in here, but you also can't erase or write over anything. And everything you've ever had is already in here. You might be thinking I am the bad guy, but *you* did these things, right?

Maciej Boniek (12)
Alness Academy, Alness

THE TRAP

I was in this dark, mucky and air-tight room. I was looking at the security cameras, watching closely to see if the two young skinny boys would return. Suddenly, from a distance, I could see the two young boys approaching my house cautiously. It was getting darker and the wind was howling. They stood in front of the large thick black door which was unlocked for a reason. After years of terrorising me, I'm finally going to get revenge on them. Slowly, they opened the door cautiously and walked straight into the room filled with poison in the air.

MacAulay Smith (13)

Alness Academy, Alness

THE THREE LITTLE PIGS

We all know the little happy story of the three little pigs and the bad wolf. But what I bet you didn't know is the real plot and the true villains of this apparent kids' story.

"Breaking news as three people wearing what seems to be pig costumes have robbed the biggest bank in the world. As we speak, the whole city's police force is on the hunt. From what we are aware of, the thieves had three safe houses and two so far have been located and destroyed. With the final house holding heavy resistance, with one cop dead."

Henry Hobbs (13)
Alness Academy, Alness

CAPTURED

A faint ringing noise in my ear. Everything became so blurry. A bunch of tall figures standing over me. Is it over? Was I finally captured? So many thoughts racing through my head. As my vision came back into focus, I saw myself handcuffed and surrounded by police and heroes I've never seen. I don't remember anything and my body is still aching. As I was chucked into the police van, I slowly started losing energy, hoping my team would finish the mission, but for now I have to focus on escaping the prison. Will I escape the prison?

Marcel Kliszcz (13)
Alness Academy, Alness

SORRY

I've always been jealous of my stepsister, Cinderella. Although I hate her, I feel bad. I have a luxurious room, the best twin ever and all the clothes I could ever want. What does Cinderella have? Nothing. As much as me and my twin are practically clones of one another, I know that Mother favours her more. And I will never understand why. I was heartbroken when I heard that Cinderella was chosen by Prince Charming to be his lovely wife. Not because I had wanted to be picked, but because I had never been given the chance to apologise.

Rosie Reilly (12)
Alness Academy, Alness

SANTA'S WORKSHOP: TWISTED TALES

Here in Santa's workshop, all my elves were working hard, making all your presents. Until one day one of our elves called Callum the Mischievous caught some sort of mysterious disease. Callum knew what happened. But he never told anyone. So he came back into work good as ever and working harder than ever before. I turned around to look at my list of naughty children and as I turned around, there was this massive bang like an explosion. I had got blown off my feet. Callum was exploding the workshop with a couple of loads of dynamite.

Hollie Morrison (12)
Alness Academy, Alness

DROWNING

All my life I've been hidden in the shadows, but now it's my chance for glory. November 1st, Jackson was born. Ever since that day, it's like I've been invisible to my parents. They've paid less attention to me and stopped caring. Jackson is three now and I've only just turned seven. I'm fed up of being ignored, so now it's time to get revenge. I came up with a plan. Late at night, I woke up to Jackson crying so I took him outside to the pool and held him under. He was screaming. Then I heard Mum shout...

Maya Macaskill (13)
Alness Academy, Alness

PETER PAN'S DEFEAT

Captain Hook and Peter Pan had one of their famous battles, again. It lasted for ages. Swords bashing, lots of crashing. There was no rest in this one. It had a weird feat to it. It looked like Captain Hook was winning? Peter looked like he was getting tired. Captain Hook was excited and thrilled. I thought he would be scared after all the times he lost, and I actually thought that the final blow was going to be from Captain Hook. And it was.

Peter Pan was defeated, and Captain Hook sailed into the distance. Never ever seen again.

Kaiden George (12)
Alness Academy, Alness

THE TRAP

Some teenage kids had found a creepy and busted old house in the woods, but what they didn't know was that it was haunted by ghosts, traps in every corner of the house (I'm thinking they're not going to escape this treacherous old house, but what do you think?). They soon entered the house to find it clean. They went back outside and looked through the window and saw it was wrecked! Went back in and it was clean. Tried going back outside, wouldn't open. It was like a trap and they had been lured in to the bait...

Dylan Colson (12)
Alness Academy, Alness

THE BACK ROOMS

I was trapped inside an elevator. I tried calling for help, but the electricity was cut off, so I tried shouting - nothing! It was almost like no one was inside the building. I tried looking for tools to see. I checked the lift hatch and came across a pair of pliers. Something crashed down into the elevator. It was a pair of wires - perfect! This meant I could get out of the elevator. I got out, but there was something weird happening. No one was there on each of the three floors. I realised I was in the back rooms...

Leon Easson (13)
Alness Academy, Alness

TWISTED TALES

Six minutes till showtime, everyone was getting ready. I was just an understudy. Why did I not get the role? I was better than her. There were just a few minutes left, everyone was just stretching and practising their jumps and turns. I saw her; there she was. I walked up to her and said I could help her stretch her feet more, she agreed so I helped her. But she would have never thought I would break her feet. *Crunch!* She was screaming in pain. Then they gave me the main role. Does this mean I am a villain?

Natalia Hadyniak (13)
Alness Academy, Alness

TERROR IN DR JACK'S HOUSE

Dr Jack was a villain in Scotland and he did not like people. He actually despised them and people wanted to help him, but Dr Jack made traps around his house. When they went to try helping him, some people got past the traps and the people who didn't get past sadly died. The people who got past went to the front door and knocked and the door creaked open. They went inside and looked around and found a basement that was really creepy. They went in and looked around and then saw something creepy. It was a man...

Cameron Taylor (12)
Alness Academy, Alness

BLACK CAT

I gently touched the fawn's forehead. It would drop down the ground motionless. "Sorry, buddy." I quietly got up to my feet and went off. I noticed a black cat in the distance. The poor thing got stuck in a bear trap. I quietly ran over. My hand reached out and the trap clamped down on my hand. Blood would pour out of my fingertips and I'd see the black cat proudly padding off. I tried to get my hand out, but I just hear the skin rip and tear. The blood stained my shoes and then gunshots...

Julia Kalbukowska (12)
Alness Academy, Alness

SNOW WHITE AND THE SEVEN DWARFS TWISTED

The story of Snow White and the Seven Dwarfs is a classic but in the real story, it is far from normal. Like the original story, the huntsman tries to kill her. She runs and finds a cottage with seven dwarfs, but these seven dwarfs make her do housework and hit her if not. The day the Evil Queen comes to give her the red poison apples Snow White knows they are poisonous, so she gives them to the seven dwarfs. Each of them died in their sleep that night and Snow White lived in the cottage happily ever after.

Amelie Robinson (12)
Alness Academy, Alness

FIREMAN: THE ORIGIN

"Not this again," I said this morning while I entered the factory for another day of work. As I was eating my lunch, I slipped and fell into the lava put. The heat was so immense. I tried screaming, but it was too late. I was already submerged in the lava. I woke up, there were police and firefighters looking down at what they thought was my dead corpse. I managed to walk out. I walked over to a cop and he caught on fire and then dropped to the floor. I ran, screaming at the top of my lungs...

Nathan Ross (12)
Alness Academy, Alness

I DID IT TO SURVIVE...

No one understood me as a kid, but one day I decided to change. I thought that crime was the way to go and then people would stop looking down on me.

Two years later, I committed several crimes like bombing banks and that, but one day I realised that crime hasn't given me what I wanted. So the next day, I went to the mall and said, "There is no more bad in me." But I guess they didn't understand because one minute later, police took me and locked me up for forty years in jail.

Jan Szymanski
Alness Academy, Alness

VICTORIOUS VILLAINS

Finally, I was about to win until it all came crashing down in front of me. I was so close to winning, but it turns out I was wrong the whole time. My first failure; I couldn't believe it. The user clicked on my spam email, entered the user and password. She was an idiot, easy to hack. All of her passwords are the same. After a couple of hours, I was able to get into her bank account. I looked around and saw that there was nothing there. In the end, I gave up. Not much of a villain after all.

Sarah Ferguson (13)
Alness Academy, Alness

THE TOWER

I was trapped. My mother came up sometimes to visit, though the day I decided to tell her I wanted to go outside, she boarded up the window. She would come each day and never come back. My only source of light became a candle and I slowly ran out of food. One day, I decided I'd had enough. I had run out of food and I needed non-artificial light. So I hit at the door for hours on end, days upon days, until finally I had done it! I was free! Others deserved to be trapped there too...

Catriona Reece (12)
Alness Academy, Alness

MOTHER GOTHEL

I never really fit into this world. My dad died when I was eleven and my mum was a drunk, so she never paid any attention to me. I learned to care for myself, just not in the right way. I stole for a living and nobody would give me a job. I went on like this for years until I finally found someone who loves me. Rapunzel loves me. She hasn't realised that I need her hair. I guess I have become a bit connected to her though. After all, I am Mother Gothel. Even at 1,000 years old!

Georgia Liscoe (12)
Alness Academy, Alness

THE EVIL MAN

A boy came to school. He looked like he didn't like it, but he said he was fine. The next day, he looked better. He asked the teacher to go to the bathroom. The teacher said no, but he went anyway. He ran to the bathroom so the teacher couldn't catch him! It was time to go home, the teacher kept him back so she could talk to him. He had a sticky bomb in his bag, so he put the bomb under the teacher's table. The timer was for ten minutes, so he ran before it blew up!

Jay Ellis (13)
Alness Academy, Alness

THE EVIL MAN

Once upon a time, there was a man in his house, watching TV. He had a son called Max and he was playing on his PC. His dad was evil. Max didn't know, so he went to the shop and he saw his dad at the car shop, getting a new car for himself.

The next day, Max was at school so his dad was doing crime at the factory, stealing cars that were worth one million pounds. He stole eleven of them in a trailer back! He stored them in his garage, then he went home to watch TV.

Jack Ellis (13)
Alness Academy, Alness

TARGET

I watched my target go inside a building to go to a party. I was going to enter through the roof. When I got there, I saw two bulky bodyguards guarding the door. I threw pebbles down the stairs and they got distracted. I entered, there were a lot of people. Most of them had the scent of cigarettes but I was trying to not get distracted. Then I went over to the bar and I saw my target. It was my brother. After that, people say I am a villain but I still think I am a hero.

Sean Ferguson (13)
Alness Academy, Alness

TWISTED TALES

One day, I was walking home alone from school when I felt a sharp pain on my back. Then I started to feel very sleepy and I fell and passed out. When I woke up, I was cold, scared and worried about myself because I was in the middle of the woods. I was running to find my way out of the woods. Suddenly, I hit my head and the place I thought was the woods turned into a white room with people watching me. They knew I could see them. They came in and I saw my parents.

Ewelina Jelewska (13)
Alness Academy, Alness

THE LIFE OF THE TUBE SOCK KILLER

Hi, I'm the Tube Sock Killer. I've been around since 2005. I wasn't always the Tube Sock Killer; I was a nice boy until my mum died and my dad became an alcoholic. My dad was abusive to me and he would have some drinks at a party or at a football game, then he started to drink every day and get more abusive and then I had enough, got a tube sock and a bin bag and killed him. The police were after me, but I got away and in 2005 I killed a mum and dad.

Lennon Maclean (13)
Alness Academy, Alness

THE VILLAIN IN THE WOODS

I am a villain who lives in the woods. I look for food and if I find food, I am going to trap it. My name is Michael. I also eat grass, trees and meat. I can be friends with humans and dogs, but not cats. Cats are like food for me. I eat them. I've been trying to get out the woods for a couple of years now, but there is all this stopping me. It's just too nice in this place. I'm going to stay here for another year. I like it here and I am a villain.

Oskar Nowak (12)
Alness Academy, Alness

THE DAY OF THE JOKER

What? Where am I? Am I the Joker? Yes, I am, so I can do a lot of stuff. Let's go and steal stuff from the bank, and Batman will probably come and get me - if he can catch me! I have a fast car and he will not get me. Wait, how is he catching up to me? Let me go in this tunnel. He is still following me. I need a way out of here. Let me block him off - oh no, that will not work! Wait, what is that? A sticky grenade? Well, am I dead?

Lewis Watt (13)
Alness Academy, Alness

THE HEART OF A VILLAIN

"Harlo... Is that you? No. It can't-"

"June?"

"I..."

"You're the villain? You're the one I've been fighting all this time? I... How?"

"I didn't know like you didn't."

"What now? I can't fight you, my love."

"Why? Why not? I'm still the villain and you're still the hero after all."

"We're... We're dating! A-and we have been for years! And you're going to give it up for what?"

"I can't just suddenly stop being who I am, not even for you."

So... So what? We're just going to break up? Are... you going to break up with me... now?"

Ellie-Mai Callender (13)

Conisborough College, Catford

THE LADY AND THE LORD

That superhero act was all a lie. I hate acting like the nice guy, but it will be worth it in the end. Suddenly, Lord Benjamin appeared in front of me. "Why can't you just leave me alone?" I shouted, wanting to kill him on the spot.
"I know who you really are, Lady Vixen. I know what you've done and what you're capable of! You've been lying to me, killing all the superheroes you can," replied Lord Benjamin.
"You could never prove it. Everyone loves me! Careful because you'll be next," I chuckled.
"But you can't. I'm your brother!"

Abi Spacey (15)
Conisborough College, Catford

WHAT JUST HAPPENED?

Finally I was about to win... But he raced, sprinted, darted nervously at me with his breath, panting like a rabid dog that had run out of water. His footsteps bashed the floor like a meteorite as he steadily gained pace like an airplane. Nothing could hinder me, nothing could annihilate me, nothing could overtake me. I briskly, rapidly, swiftly grasped my sword and with one attack, he collapsed like a building in an earthquake. He was screaming quietly and slowly, before his erratic heartbeat came to a gruesome, grisly, ghastly end. I left the petrified forest without any hesitation.

Dilvesh Gopinath (14)
Conisborough College, Catford

IF ONLY WE WERE US

Finally, I was about to win! All of my hard work paying off!
"On your knees for me?" I laugh sarcastically, pulling his
shivering chin up to face me. He flinches; must be in pain. "It
didn't have to be like this," I remind him innocently
"Just do it!" he stutters out, choking on blood. Glancing back
to look at him, his eyes still glistened like the day we met.
I'm standing there, silently, gun to his head. One bullet to
end it all. Yet something deep down holds onto us before all
of this. When we were still together...

Ronnie Donnelly (13)
Conisborough College, Catford

HIS MISTAKE

He darted down the busy road. People stopped to stare, but that was the least of his concerns. His past was finally catching up with him. After being the villain for so long, he wasn't used to running away. His shoes were wet from the number of puddles he had stepped in. Hastily, he rounded a corner and began sprinting down an unlit alleyway as the image of a woman flashed through his mind. He glanced over his shoulder. That was his mistake. In front of him, the woman appeared. Knife in her hand.

"You couldn't have thought I'd forgotten."

Naomi Okojie (14)
Conisborough College, Catford

THE BETRAYAL

Our plan was working but he betrayed me. My family died for this. I thought they were the enemy; I was wrong. Screaming, panicking, begging for their lives and I let it happen. He burned them alive. I pretended not to care, all for the Reverand. I wanted to get revenge. Who would listen to a little girl?
The night was long until I saw him again. Struggling, sweating, screaming, I dangled above the glowing orange flames. I was accused of witchcraft. I tried to escape, cutting my fingers. He told me, "Don't be afraid, it will be over soon."

Abby Stevens (13)
Conisborough College, Catford

TIRED OF BEING GOOD

What happens when you become tired of being 'good'? What *really* is the point when it is already expected of you? No big deal. Right? You could save the world and still it's *never* enough. Enough for the public eye. They give credit to those lazying, and leave people like me. My loving heart once overflowing with love was taken for granted. Now it's guarded with black ice. But you can't live without being evil at least once. You must enjoy the thrill. And while you plot, you're congratulated for not creating chaos...

Shayanne Barrie (14)
Conisborough College, Catford

THE BEING

I did it to survive. I had to kill him before he killed us. Blood curdled down his throat. I watched him suffer in pain. Raising this boy like my son, I couldn't bear to see his blood spill. I wailed with regret. This wouldn't have happened if his people didn't attack. Lurking through the forest, my eyes glimpsed a blue-eyed blonde being.

From that day, I had watched him grow into a brave boy. Things took a twist. I had explained to him that he mustn't leave town or they'll know. I couldn't continue to explain what happened.

Rovaughn Halstead (13)
Conisborough College, Catford

FREDDY FAZBEAR'S PIZZERIA

This is the story about a killer who works as a security guard at a pizza place called Freddy Fazbear's Pizzeria. His name was William Afton and now he rots in Hell. It all started in 1987 when five children went missing, but the truth is *he* did it. William put on a yellow bunny suit that he took from a mysterious location. He lured the children to the secret room. When they were in the room, William shut the door, taking the suit off, brought a knife out, slowly stabbing, blood bursting out, splashing on the walls...

Jimmy Husseyin (13)
Conisborough College, Catford

ALL EYES ON ME

A glass shard appears in front of me. Crystal clear. Almost angelic. *Smash!* Fractured is a bottle upon the floor - or so they thought. I observe the glamorous structure and admire it in all its bearing. The reflection of sea glimmers in the sun. Suddenly, this shattered. A sinister smile upon my face. Blood tints the streets. Pandemonium. Chaos. Catastrophe. The world will recognise me. Never will I be in the shadows. All eyes will be on me. Will you accept me now, sister? Her soulless eyes stare. Do you accept me?

Blessing Osahan (13)
Conisborough College, Catford

PAIN! SORROW!

I always felt different to my dysfunctional family, but I never knew why. Not until my malicious mother told me that she had an affair with another man that led to my birth. The 500+ years I've lived and she never thought to tell me. All the abuse I went through for being different; pain! Sorrow! For what? My stepdad was always abusive. No wonder she didn't tell me. But still, I need to know. An awful childhood. All the bloodbaths he caused. All of my trapped trauma tossed around for his own amusement. Pain! Sorrow!

Ellie Dorey (13)
Conisborough College, Catford

REVENGE

I still haven't forgotten. It has been ten years since my mother was murdered. I have been planning ever since my mother was murdered by a heartless she-beast. My mother was a nice, beautiful, perfect woman who did not deserve to die. I hate you, Amy Thomson. I cannot wait to kill her; she deserves everything that is coming to her. She does not deserve to live after what she has done. I cannot wait to see the blood leaking from her neck while she screams for help, but no one will help her. Amy Thompson, you will die.

Phillipa Davidson (14)
Conisborough College, Catford

PARANOID SCHIZOPHRENIA

I was in my demoralized house, in my room, in my closet. I hear voices in my head. They count to me. They understand they talk to me. *They talk to me.* He ruined me. Damaged me. I did what I did to survive. Help me. The blood won't come off. He was spreading rumours, saying mean things. I just want my brother back. He helped me. My mummy cared for me. My daddy taught me. I need them. The man ruined me; won't let me get away. Won't let me go. I don't feel like doing this anymore. Goodbye...

Anthony Heard (13)
Conisborough College, Catford

EMPTY...

I limped around the school. I wasn't hurt, but it felt like I'd been stabbed millions of times. Ever since they moved away, I've had no reason to live. No will to live. No way to live... Maybe if someone had come to my rescue or someone paid attention to me, I wouldn't have turned out this way. I halted in my tracks as I saw my victim. My prey. My food. I didn't like doing this, but no one really cared. I took the prey's personal property as it scampered away. Why oh why was I the bully?

Iyanu Stephens (13)
Conisborough College, Catford

WHAT I DO ON MY DAY OFF!

I'm having a day off from saving people's lives. I'm Dracula if you didn't know. I ran a nice warm bubble bath and jumped in. I was relaxing; I've never felt this calm before. I was relaxed when I received a call from my oldest friend asking to hang out. I met her in the park and we grabbed ice cream and had a chat about how our lives have been since we last met. We met our other friend and went to a coffee shop. We said goodbye and went home. I got home and had a hot chocolate.

Paige Gregson-Lloyd (13)
Conisborough College, Catford

ROARING FLAMES

I did it to survive. He wasn't supposed to see me yet. I told him to meet me at 5 o'clock because I had urgent matters to attend to. But he caught me standing over a fire that took away all the lives that ruined mine. Jan was one of the innocent ones until the flames roared. He tried to run and stop me and I had to hide the evidence. Then I looked over at him and realised he was next. He fell over a rock, half alive, gasping and suffering for me to help him. He's done!

Madina Shahin (14)
Conisborough College, Catford

HOME INVADER

It was a murky and dim night. I was in my house lonesome; I was on my phone. Then I got a message. 'I can see you.' I began to hear crashing at my door, then my doorbell went off. I ran to hide in a secret passage in my house. Whoever it was I didn't want to know. He came in, then through a hole I saw his face. His face was burnt to a crisp and disfigured. He started looking everywhere. I began to shed tears. I was terrified. My phone went off. He looked!

Robert Heard (13)
Conisborough College, Catford

THEM!

I had to make up for what I had done. Tables were turned, drinks were spilt and the blame was on... them. I tried all I could to make it up to them and yet it was not good enough. I cleaned and cried and it still wasn't good enough. A few days passed and I'd done everything I could to help, only to realise I was them. They were me. What did I do to deserve this punishment? What did I do? Was I this bad person? Was I the reason for all of this... or not?

Tia Lye-Corne (13)
Conisborough College, Catford

ELSA'S DEMISE

"I never really belonged with my twelve brothers in the Southern Isles. That's why I journeyed to Arendelle. My intention is to become king," Hans explained as his servants washed Elsa's clothes. The plan to marry her had failed. The only form of redemption for such treachery was her death. Seizing the king's sword, Hans stormed towards the unexpecting, clueless queen. Laughing menacingly, he pierced her skin between her shoulder blades. The queen fell, lifeless. "Finally, I will..." The realisation dawned, the weight of his actions fell heavily upon his seared conscience. Redemption was found by falling on his sword.

Amelia Dalzell (11)
Crumlin Integrated College, Crumlin

COVID

I had to make up for what I'd done. COVID had arrived, spreading like wildfire... COVID hit like a bomb, people dropping like flies. There were multiple deaths, people got sick, hospitals became busier. Doctors under pressure, nurses under-staffed, the NHS overwhelmed. Testing became increasingly popular, lockdowns became increasingly frequent. No one allowed into the country or out. People became depressed, anxious and scared. The innocent lost their lives because of this dreaded disease. Families fought and fell out, finances stretched with furlough schemes. When would it end? This was not my intention when I created this bio-weapon.

Darragh Close (14)
Crumlin Integrated College, Crumlin

DRACULA

When Harker arrives in Transylvania, the locals react with terror after he discloses his destination: Castle Dracula. Though this unsettles him slightly, he continues onward. The ominous howling of wolves rings through the air as he arrives triumphantly at the castle. Meeting Dracula, Harker acknowledges his appearance to be pale, gaunt and strange. Tentatively, he is shown to his room. A nervous shave results in Harker cutting his neck. The smell of blood wafts into the air, sending Dracula and his fiends into a feeding frenzy. Realising his plight, Harker attempts to escape, being pursued by three vampires, including Dracula...

Ranim Al Homsi (14)
Crumlin Integrated College, Crumlin

THE COUNTER

"Finally, I was about to win." Well, that's what Medusa thought. She already lost the battle; she didn't know about hero Perseus' plan.

Let's go back to the start of it all. Medusa is a Gorgon, a girl with snakes as hair, and wings. Hero Perseus is a good who got help from Athena who gave him a mirror shield.

Well, let's resume. "You would be nice to add to my collection." She jumped with joy.

"Well, I don't give up without a fight." Medusa stared intensely as she turned to stone.

"How are you?" Hero Perseus smiled with might...

Kyle Canning (12)
Crumlin Integrated College, Crumlin

WHAT IF HITLER WON WORLD WAR II?

Finally, I was about to win this wretched war and bring peace to the people of Europe. My ambitions were nearly accomplished: world domination. A small island nation stood in my way. Britain was nearly conquered, my invasion of Scotland was swift and startling. The Romans hadn't even accomplished my exploits. My war machine turned anti-clockwise as my invincible army swept through Ireland and Wales. England was the last stronghold. Maximum pain and suffering must be exerted upon that puny, pesky nation. A new era is dawning, one with Germany at its centre. Is anyone capable of stopping me? No!

Ciaran Creber (12)
Crumlin Integrated College, Crumlin

THE FIERCE FLAMING FIRE

That superhero act was all a lie. On a cool night, by the orange glow of the fire, we rushed to my grandfather's home. His barn had caught fire, it was ancient. Firemen told us to stand nearby to witness the pumping water eliminate the flames. Water arrived from our beloved creek, it was sucked dry. Our drinking water vanished. The flames stirred memories of past traumatic events. I had the melted skin to prove it. It was suspicious that this barn erupted into flames again; perhaps it was cursed. *Where is Grandfather?* I pondered.

"He's consumed," a voice replied...

Omar Shrouf (16)

Crumlin Integrated College, Crumlin

MISSION FAILED?

I had to make up for what I'd done. After I failed my final assassination, Luther sent his highly armed men after me. Afraid, I cowered into a corner and began to rapidly shake with unwelcomed goosebumps dotted all over my skin in patterns. I bust into the rustic run-down building's door and rummaged through to find either a weapon or help. I began searching under beds, sofas, tables, you name it. I'd found a decent hiding spot, but it was too late. My earpiece was connected to Luther's services, therefore, frustratingly, they could track me down. *Wait!* No...!

Daniel Allen (12)
Crumlin Integrated College, Crumlin

MAYHEM MOLTEN

It was a beautiful day! The sun was shining. Until... a loud menacing roar shot out of the volcano and smoke filled the sky. Parents were crying and praying for their children. Everyone was evacuating. There was no way out. The Beeching family ran to a nearby cave, hoping it would shelter them from the great evil demolishing the town. Lava started melting through the stone wall of the cave. The Beechings were frightened but couldn't do anything! The last thing everyone heard was the innocent cries of pain from the Beechings' flesh being burned off by molten-like liquid.

Isabelle Beeching (12)
Crumlin Integrated College, Crumlin

THE BETRAYAL

I had to make up for what I'd done. Once best friends, but now they are enemies, Dracula and Crimson had the perfect relationship except for the fact that Dracula was a vampire. It was the first day of school, everyone crowded Dracula. He was so full of himself, he forgot about Crimson. This carried on for months. Crimson was sick of being treated like dirt. "You don't care about me!" Crimson screamed. Dracula stared at Crimson, his eyes glowed and in a flash they both collapsed...

Dracula woke up in a grubby prison cell. He'd killed his best friend.

Erin Mathieson (12)
Crumlin Integrated College, Crumlin

HACKED OFF!

Plotting for two years. I'm scared. I'm going to hack into the White House! I want to earn a reputation to be in Hacker Utopia. Through the firewall and then hack the mainframe. The password generator is speeding through the combinations like the speed of light. Bingo! I'm in! I can't believe it. All my rivals have been trying to get in for years and I did it!
Bang! I freeze.
FBI?
I scramble to turn everything off. A familiar voice... The neighbour.
"Have you seen my dog?"
I log back in but nothing. I had blown it!

Darren Lam (11)
Crumlin Integrated College, Crumlin

MEDUSA: LOST HOPE

I was sobbing uncontrollably, shaking as the stone bodies surrounded me. Wondering, *how could I do this?* I walked around my temple, staring at the many candles and gifts the women left me. Suddenly, I heard a loud crash! I slowly walked to the stairs, noticing the light from afar. I heard Hercules' voice saying, "Oh, Medusa, where are you?"
He appeared with a lantern, hunting for me. He found me. I spoke out confidently, "Hercules! Leave! I want nothing to do with you!"
He pulled out something. I opened my eyes... I was frozen.

Eva Barr (13)
Crumlin Integrated College, Crumlin

FIVE YEARS

Finally, I was about to win a battle that would cost everything. "Five years!" I cried. "It ends now," I mumbled under my breath before leaping off the large rock that I was standing on. As I swung my weapon at the ground, just then he rolled to the side, evading my attack. "*Stop fighting, it's over!*" I howled. He stood up with great pain.
"Not yet!" he exclaimed whilst cracking his knuckles, he then took off in a sprint. I had injured my leg in battle, so I was unable to catch him. I still haven't found him.

Phillip Bamford (12)
Crumlin Integrated College, Crumlin

UNCONDITIONAL SCHEMING

"I never really belonged in Asgard. I was always... different."
Perhaps it was his love of pranks or his magic. His father,
Odin, always made him feel... inferior or lonely. Though his
mother, Freyja, was always kind to him. Maybe the only
reason he hurt people was that he just wanted to be
noticed. He was known as 'Loki the trickster'. He was
planning revenge now; he was going to make them finally
notice. Odin and all the people of Asgard. Loki never really
put this much thought into his plans, but he wanted this
scheme to succeed, unlike others...

Georgina Cormican (12)
Crumlin Integrated College, Crumlin

VICKY'S STORY

Vicky was so confused. Her mother told her that she will never see her father again. With tears flooding her face, Vicky ran away, into the dark, searching for him. She searched for her father. She got so furious that she decided to destroy anyone who tried to stop her. She killed twenty-five people and kept searching. Vicky was in the centre of the village. About to be burned, she decided to confess to the villagers that the reason she murdered people was because her father betrayed her. The villagers forgave her and the rest is history. Vicky the vulture.

Faith Sole (12) & Calum
Crumlin Integrated College, Crumlin

CRIME PAYS

On that fateful stormy night eight years ago, my dad's shop was viciously raided by a madman unable to suffer the consequences of his actions. I lie in wait for him, like a cougar stalking its prey. I spot the rough robber from miles away and soon pursue him through the dark, cold and dirty alleyways. We soon tussle, wrestle and fight like animals in the dirty, depressing and filthy streets. The man-mountain soon yields and lies on the floor from exhaustion. The sirens get louder, not knowing the real truth behind the madness caused. Please believe me!

Zach Moorman (14)
Crumlin Integrated College, Crumlin

WHAT WOULD YOU CHOOSE?

I've roamed the halls of this maze, trapped, with no escape... forced to eat unfortunate victims for my master's cruel and twisted ways. Shunned by all for being an abomination when their king had no soul. The day began with chanting (sound travels far in this place). A new tribute was trapped with me. Pity.

I brace myself for the task of hunting my meal and a haunting slam vibrates along the endless tunnels. I begin my hunt. As I follow the lost soul, I contemplate, is this worth it? But I have no choice! It's a kill-or-be-killed world!

Jorge Mullan-Starr (14)
Crumlin Integrated College, Crumlin

FOUL SINGERS

Finally, I was about to win. I heard a loud sound. It was *those* vile singers! The noise was hurting my ears, giving me a headache. They did not stop singing and irritating me. They needed to go, so I hatched a plan to get rid of them for good. As they were singing like a pack of animals, I walked towards them furiously. "Come with me for some Christmas fun!" I exclaimed menacingly. Foolishly, they followed me into a dark, deserted cave. The singers were confused. Gleefully, I pushed a boulder in front of the cave. I had succeeded.

Luca Costello (12)
Crumlin Integrated College, Crumlin

THE HUNT

Finally, I was about to win the challenge of best captain. I got so close, then my arch-nemesis swooped in and stole it from me. From that day forward, I vowed to get revenge. Heading back to my top-secret underground bunker, I contemplated how to exact my revenge. Then it occurred to me, a most terrible thought, *he must die and I will take the trophy for myself*. I rallied the troops and prepared my ship with stockpiles of guns shot and grappling hooks. A sense of pride filled my heart. "Look out, world, I came to get revenge."

Michelle Kelly (14)
Crumlin Integrated College, Crumlin

THE TERRIFYING MURDER

After today, I felt as if the world didn't want me anymore. I turned around and smashed five bottles against my head. The voices were pulsing through my brain, becoming deeper and darker. Trapped in my own thoughts, the door knocked. Gingerly, I opened it. My wife was standing there; she had just murdered our son! Her violence was terrifying. I know how bad she treated me; I couldn't bear it any longer. A rush came over me. Enraged, I picked up the glass vase, raising it high for the fatal blow. I'm no piece of dirt to be abused.

Chelsy Rainey (14)
Crumlin Integrated College, Crumlin

REDEMPTION

I had to make up for what I had done for I, the king of all, have granted a mortal access to our ancient scriptures. I must make it right, I must stop him and demolish him to keep my fellow gods safe. Swiftly, I transformed into a body of an eagle. Flying towards this earthling, I swooshed past and swiftly chopped off his head. Once that was completed, I burned down his feeble mortal village, reclaiming the terrible knowledge I granted him. To ensure no one spoke of this, I killed everyone. I only have my fellow gods' understanding.

Josh Megarry-Hewitt (13)
Crumlin Integrated College, Crumlin

THE YOUNG TEEN AGAINST THE OLDER TEENS

I had to make up for what I'd done... I stood there, standing against a creviced wall in a fatal, ghoulish alleyway. Suddenly, I heard cursed laughing sprinting into my ears. I peered around the corner and saw two girls and three boys. All their hoodies over their faces and not a glimpse to see. One girl stood outside, she looked suspicious, so I walked close to her. I tried to talk to her, but she looked down and ignored me.

I strangled her and ran into a demonic, gloomy forest. I peeked out to see flashing lights and sirens.

Freya Mullen (13)
Crumlin Integrated College, Crumlin

WHO IS THE WINNER?

Sirens screaming all around. A living bomb escaping, putting everyone in danger. All their nightmares coming true as it has escaped... People begin to panic as they hear of this terrible beast and its evil plans. Suddenly, an almighty crash echoes around town. Smoke fills the air. Out walks a muscular man here to save the world. The evil creature hears the news and doesn't know what to do. *Crash!* The hero bursts through the door. They fight all day and night. Back and forth until a winner emerges. But who will it be?

Mason Lovell (13)
Crumlin Integrated College, Crumlin

THE GRINCH

High up on a stormy mountain lived the Grinch who hates Christmas. He was bullied at school for what he looked like. He had green fur all over him. He finally had enough. "I must educate these people!" he said with a groan.

At that moment, the Grinch's school was on, he taught them not to care what people think of them; not to care if they look different and that everyone is unique. The Whos loved him. They were happier than they were before. Whoville was a much happier place. They felt safer with the Grinch.

Brooke Gilmore (12)

Crumlin Integrated College, Crumlin

THE BACKSTORY OF A STONE-EYED MONSTER

I watched as my life flashed before my eyes. Minerva turned me into a monster. *What did I do?* I thought. What happened? I was a gorgeous maiden and now I am a green slimy snake. I need to find Minerva to explain her mistake, although I'm unable to leave this cave. I have been cursed. I will wait for freedom. I slept long nights until an unexpected guest came. Perseus intruded, as I slept, to behead me! That night, I was killed with no hesitation.

I am Medusa and that is how I died from an accused crime scene.

Olivia Belmar (11)
Crumlin Integrated College, Crumlin

THE DEVIL'S STORY

I'm having a day off from being Satan's little puppet. He likes having control of everyone around him. That's why everyone fears him. Satan is almost human-like, apart from his deathly-like wings. He likes to tell his followers that God doesn't exist, and this was the only way to go. For fun, he likes to drag down undead souls from the other side. Hell isn't a very nice place. When you look around, you just see lava. So next time you might want to be nice before you end up down under with the Devil himself.

Lucie Watson (11)
Crumlin Integrated College, Crumlin

BLOODBATH REDEMPTION

I had to make up for what I'd done. That tragic mistake. I killed innocent people!
Sweating profusely, I jolt up from my dream; I often had flashbacks. Sarah, my love, questioned why I was so on edge, scared... How could I tell her the truth? Frankly, the military was horrific, so I bailed before we were shipped off. To be honest, I hadn't thought it through. I went home like I hadn't left home. When I did, I got hounded by Sarah about why I left. The lies... They are killing me! I have to fix this, but how?

Katy-Mae Hopkins (14)
Crumlin Integrated College, Crumlin

THE BATTLE OF THE EVIL

Finally, I was about to win. The Wicked Witch of the West had a gigantic wound in her left arm, her good arm, from when I struck her with lightning. She screamed angrily, "It's not over yet, Maleficent!"

I swiftly replied with, "Not yet, but it will soon be." All of a sudden, a house fell on the witch!

Two years later and I am now getting really sick. I got a letter from the hospital saying I must hand my crown of horns to the witch's daughter and when I died, my soul helped everyone...

Katie-Rose Wallace (12)

Crumlin Integrated College, Crumlin

DOCTOR OCTOPUS' VICTORIOUS VILLAINY

I'm having a day off from committing petty crimes. It's time for me to seek revenge for my six-year-old daughter. I am a known criminal, but if I change ID, I think it'll be safe. My name is Doctor Octopus and I have created an invention that has never been used before; it has eight robot arms bulging out of my back, with sensitive alarms to help me stay aware of any superheroes. Nothing will spoil my devious plan. There is one puny hero called 'Spider-Man'. He will ruin my plan, or at least try to...

Nathan Belmar (12)
Crumlin Integrated College, Crumlin

FRIDAY THE 13TH, NEXT SUMMER

I'm having a day off.

I crawled out of my tent at 3am on Friday the 13th. My black hair shimmered in the moonlight. I saw a door open, I walked over and saw rotting floorboards; stepping on a rotted one would be the stuff of nightmares. Little did I know it already had begun. I noticed a figure wearing a hockey mask, bearing a hatchet. I sprinted for the others. Realising I was being followed, I leapt up the porch, into a hut, and noticed I was trapped. I jumped out a window and fell into the eerie lake...

Lorenzo Lauro (11)

Crumlin Integrated College, Crumlin

THE FAKER

The superhero act was all a lie. Serbious was a hellhound. He was set up by a hero in disguise. His name was Loki, the god of deception. He was actually a villain who set up Serbious. He was stuck, protecting the gates of Hell. Loki actually killed the man. When Serbious was protecting the gates, he met an old man who said he would give him tremendous power. So Serbious went to fight Loki. When Serbious got there, he was ready to fight but Loki had already left the village because he was too scared of Serbious...

Declan Duvey (11)
Crumlin Integrated College, Crumlin

THE HIDDEN TRUTH

That superhero act was all a lie. My nickname is Nightwing, known as Daniel Arthur. I was an orphan. My parents died when I was three and I grew up in Texas. I was very helpful. I loved to stop crime, but suddenly I got mixed emotions and chose the disgraceful way. So from then on, no one trusted in me and I was a wanted target for the police. Suddenly, I was cut, battered and bruised after what I had risked. I really did want to change, but I can't. It's too late for me. Suddenly, I was caught...

Scott Boston (13)
Crumlin Integrated College, Crumlin

LIFE, DEATH, WAR AND VENGEANCE: MY LEGACY

My men lie dead, spread out across the field... They bombed us! I told them we were fine, we were a well-oiled machine, a war machine! We would've won the battle, but no, they had to cover it up. The damn trees are on fire. My entire platoon is dead, stars falling from the sky. The hot ashes of my brothers in arms, may they rest in peace. No more orders, no holding back, no more listening! I'll fight this war my way, on my terms. My damn life; this is my vengeance. *My war!*

Geordan Mullen (14)
Crumlin Integrated College, Crumlin

UNDER THE SEA

I'm having a day off from stealing voices from mermaids. It's a very tricky job. I'm going to kick my tentacles and go to the spa to get a mud mask, massage and sit in a hot tub. Then I am going to go for a swim in the posh area of the sea because their houses are much nicer than my lair before going home and eating some mussels. I can't wait to go to my bed and get a good night's sleep because in the morning all my evil plans will go back into action...

Holly Knox (14)
Crumlin Integrated College, Crumlin

TEACHER OF THE YEAR

Finally, I was about to win. Untightening the bolts on the scenery for the school's extravaganza sealed Miss Jacob's fate. However, Jason Willis I felt guilty about. Changing dates and times for the upcoming championship's play schedule was harsh. Incompetent. I knew Nathan set up his experiments before lesson; an extra heap of iodine ensured. His surprised face, hair and anything within five feet glowed a glorious violet. An uneasy pang emerged. I hadn't planned on tipping the scales quite so much. Standing next to the podium, I felt *odd*. Not triumphant. Unnervingly *they* stood. Shoulder to shoulder, quietly smiling...

Phoebie Allen (12)
Great Yarmouth Charter Academy, Great Yarmouth

THE VIEWS OF A GENIUS

Almost everyone called me strange, an abnormality. I was smart. They were slaves. I was fourteen when I killed my parents. An accident, obviously. The plan was never to hurt them, but once a flame sparks, it devours everything. That's when I realised murder brought the freedom people desperately needed in their 'lives'. Everyone lives and dies. It's depressing, but we're mortal. You'll recall that I said almost everyone. It was true, almost everyone did. However, there was one kid at school who appreciated my genius. Anya Mort. Her name meant 'death'. Suitable considering what happened next in the story.

Beth Noble (14)
Great Yarmouth Charter Academy, Great Yarmouth

TWO-FACED DESIRE

"A tragedy, no?" the villain divulged, laughing pitilessly at the frail and wounded woman before him. He, a devil in disguise. She, a merciful angel. He simply craved her company. She simply loved too easily. The contrast between the disconnect of their mind was too dismal and agonising. The angle left shattered, dying amongst the corpses of others, while her so-called 'lover' looked down at her, repulse covering his features. She's always regarded him as a blessing, but his words had pierced her skin deeply like a passing bullet. Yet he continued, "But there's always beauty in a tragedy."

Iris Vaz (13)
Great Yarmouth Charter Academy, Great Yarmouth

WHITE STALK

Report file of the White Stalk Killer:
The White Stalk terrorised the town of Yarmouth from 1932 to 1939. He would manipulate people into trusting him, kill them at their weakest. When the first murder of many came through, people were terrified of the non-forgiving murderer. He left white stalks nearby every murder. Authorities had no leads on him for most of the murders, only non-helpful evidence. When the Second World War started, he took the life of Desmond Brown, the last of the murders. After this, he had an inactive life. He just disappeared?
Report closed.

Kaiden Carapinha (12)
Great Yarmouth Charter Academy, Great Yarmouth

THE MASSACRE

Having no mercy, he licked the blood that trickled down his pale face and stepped on the corpses that overlapped each other and were bleeding a dark, sour, malevolent liquid. With no hesitation, I clutched my nose as the rotten and decayed smell of the infested bodies progressed into my lungs. A city that previously contained laughter, merriment and smiles was now a black silent wasteland. With a stone-cold heart, he whispered, "Unlucky." Suffocating in the thick contaminated fog, I held my wound that leaked endless blood. I took one last gasp of air, closed my eyes and waited...

Cristina Gabrieli (13)
Great Yarmouth Charter Academy, Great Yarmouth

FORBIDDEN LOVE!

Harley Quinn, a well-respected psychologist at the New York Institute for the Medically Insane, fell in love with her patient Jack Napier. As we all know, it's forbidden and unprofessional. One day, at Jack's apartment, he convinced Harley to help him escape so they could be together.
Believing all the things Jack was telling her, Harley devised a plan to help Jack escape. The night of Jack's escape, a very naive, loved-up Harley gave Jack copies of the master keys and a location for meeting her.
Midnight came and Harley was waiting for the love that never came.

Paris Jonas-Smith (11)
Great Yarmouth Charter Academy, Great Yarmouth

LEO'S BACKSTORY

Leo was a very intelligent and rational individual who was strong-willed. He went to a university called University of Oxford and got a good education and became an investment banker. He got greedy and used his mother's possessions for financial collateral in his investments. He was scared he couldn't pay off what he owed. He offered his mother's house and restaurant, but unfortunately the investments failed, putting him in a debt of £6 million! Everything Leo did he did for his mum. He couldn't find the courage to return to his mum, so he joined a game...

Rumer Skidmore (13)
Great Yarmouth Charter Academy, Great Yarmouth

WHY THE ALIENS SEEK REVENGE ON EARTH

There was a wall in the solar system from about 100,000,000 years ago that surrounded all the planets from the sun to Neptune. One day, an asteroid that was carrying alien DNA hit the wall, though it bounced off and hit back at Mars.

Over 1,000,000 years the asteroid developed into billions of little aliens. Though because of the damage, Mars was on its last legs. The aliens saw what had happened. They wished it could have hit Earth instead of their newly beloved planet Mars. They started to take this personally and began their master plan to invade Earth...

Isobel Tann (12)

Great Yarmouth Charter Academy, Great Yarmouth

THE DEMON BARBER

My life was perfect, my family I adored. Everything was ripped apart by the corrupt Judge Turpin. My wife and child murdered without a thought. Absorbing the terror and shock, an overwhelming urge for revenge controlled my being. I became a barber with a cut-throat razor. Customers came through my door. Then Turpin took the chair one day and my chance, by chance, became real. The blade took over from my resistance, risking a capture. The blood flowed from his body, along with his life. Thus the demon was born. My job was done, but this wasn't the end yet...

Emilee Sweeney (12)
Great Yarmouth Charter Academy, Great Yarmouth

DON'T TRUST EVERYTHING YOU SEE ON SOCIAL MEDIA

Some events shape people for better or for worse. Personally speaking, my series of events brutally changed my life. Vlogging was supposed to help, but it led to something different instead.

I turned off my camera. My thoughts went wild. I had to calm down. But how? I knew exactly how. I could... add a new crime to my episode list. But not through research. Through personal experience. I grabbed my knife and headed outside. I just needed to be careful. Very careful. Imagine if they found out who did all this. That won't be today though. Or will it?

Kelsie Stringer (14)

Great Yarmouth Charter Academy, Great Yarmouth

TO THESEUS

Philza knew I messed up. I knew I shouldn't have said that to a teenager, but you, Tommy, betrayed me for people who exiled you. The voices were loud, loud enough I couldn't think straight, couldn't control myself. I'm a pawn to people to keep something safe, like the Minotaur. In the labyrinth, I was known to be a monster. Only after blood as that is what the voices cried for. Though now I hope that my best and only friend's son will have a good ending. I'm sorry, Theseus, for how I acted to you in my lifetime.
-Protesilaus.

Emma Lilley (14)
Great Yarmouth Charter Academy, Great Yarmouth

I'LL NEVER KILL AGAIN BECAUSE...

He was dead. There was no doubt about it. Lorelai had killed someone and never wished to again. Her entire life in that household with nothing but the rats and bugs to accompany her, Lorelai could only stare at the life draining out of her father's eyes, a knife puncturing his flesh. Her father let out a broken sob and slumped to the floor. The pounding in her head and her trembling blood-covered fingers informed Lorelai that she'd unleashed a monster. Lorelai had killed someone and never wished to again because she liked it a little too much...

Eda Revuckaite (13)
Great Yarmouth Charter Academy, Great Yarmouth

IT WAS ALL A LIE

Her plan is in motion. Her phone rings.
"Have you got the package?" a deep, intimidating voice replies. "I'm sending it to the warehouse."
When she gets to the warehouse, there is no package. She sees a silhouette in the distance. "Where is the package?" The intimidating voice replies, "There is no package. You have been living a dream, your life is a lie and without this lie you are nothing. This is all a set-up. Your friends are fake and your family are too. Your life is a *lie!*"

Rachael Bailey (13)
Great Yarmouth Charter Academy, Great Yarmouth

THE SURPRISE TO GODS

One day, a big, hairy, three-eyed monster came along and rained havoc on Enyo's favourite city. Now Enyo loved destruction, but not to her safe haven. She came down from the sunny sky, turning it grey, and destroyed the mighty beast that fought as if a wounded lion. They fought for hours on end. But the beast could not be defeated. Enyo had a plan. She would get her father, Zeus, to help her. Zeus agreed and off they went, not knowing that it was actually Aphrodite. Zeus could sense it was her. Enyo and Zeus tremendously helped Aphrodite.

Patricia Staff (11)
Great Yarmouth Charter Academy, Great Yarmouth

IS IT THE PRO-HEROES TO BLAME?

Hey, Tenko here. When I was younger, I found a picture of my grandma. My father hated that I'd found it. I escaped to the garden and hugged my dog. It started to decay. My sister ran outside. I touched the floor and she fell through! All of them died that day. I walked through town. A woman looked at me, but my affected eyes must've scared her. I prepared myself for a night of sleeping rough, but AFO found me.

I'm older now, but that day still haunts me. Do *you* think I'm horrendous, or is it the pro-heroes?

Ella Ellis (13)
Great Yarmouth Charter Academy, Great Yarmouth

THE GRENCH

In a land far, far away, there was a village being terrorised by a mighty villain. Day by day, the citizens of Glasmere would be living their mundane lives. Children would play tag and hopscotch on the roads, and adults would drive home from work. In Glasmere, there was one person who stood out, the Grench. He was the youngest of five brothers. The Grench was a different person to the people of Glasmere. He lived away from the town square. He lived on a dark, steep cliff, isolated. Nobody ever expected the Grench to be who he was today...

Daisy Hills (11)
Great Yarmouth Charter Academy, Great Yarmouth

THE BEAST'S TRUE CREATOR

LeFou is a young man who works for the Duke of Rhone on his huge estate. He witnesses the duke's cruelty first-hand and wishes for him to be punished. His wish is granted one day when a witch comes and punishes the duke for his cruelty. After his transformation into a hideous beast, he appears to become a better person. But one day, after having her father taken by the beast, a young woman arrives at the castle and threatens to undo the curse. LeFou does everything in his power to manipulate Gaston into killing the beast for him...

Marcio Rocha (14)
Great Yarmouth Charter Academy, Great Yarmouth

THE REVENGE PLAN

After all this time, it was him who I couldn't kill. It was on my last nerve. I would have given up, but I couldn't. My last plan couldn't fail. This plan was greater than any other. I could never forgive my brother after that horrid night. I was never the villain. He was. He was the one who murdered our father, though I never understood why. Who do the public think they are, calling him a hero?

Now, let's put the past aside. Was twenty-three years ago. My plan failed. He won. I'm just here for revenge.

Imogen Butcher (12)
Great Yarmouth Charter Academy, Great Yarmouth

AFTER EVER AFTER

I still haven't forgotten the amount of civilians I killed that day. For me, it was an achievement to add to my cabinet of people dead. Knowing I never finished one of the civilians that day, I found out that one still lived who I never decided to kill. So I made a mission to make an end to this civilian's life, making him die by a stab to the heart, knowing it would be another achievement in the cabinet.

Over the days, I've always remembered the people I killed. I still never forget the blood-splatter around.

Mason Pitts-Cross (12)
Great Yarmouth Charter Academy, Great Yarmouth

DEADLY ENCOUNTERS

I was minding my own business, when a human came wandering into my territory. I pondered for a while then decided to mess with them. I whispered menacing things through the bushes and set trees on fire. I showed myself running through the trees, they looked horrified. That made me self-conscious about not being human. Most people are scared of me. I smiled to myself as they ran home.

Ten years passed, a human was chasing me, brandishing a knife. I tripped over a log and felt the knife go through my heart. It was all over.

Phoebe Carter (13)
Great Yarmouth Charter Academy, Great Yarmouth

DEATHLY STORY

He stumbled down the stairs, Noir laughed. "Here is my story, as promised, Alex. Once I was a little girl, I was visited by Death. He promised a fraction of a lifetime, causing me to love the need to kill. Even my parents couldn't escape my wrath. Now I will kill you, my 100th victim!"
Alex turned around and shot her. Noir bled to death. Alex walked away in pride. Noir then began to chant a spell. She rose.
"You thought this would be the end? You were wrong, Alex. *I can never die!*"

Scarlett Hudson (11)
Great Yarmouth Charter Academy, Great Yarmouth

THE GEMINI COVEN

Yes, I was a villain, but the reason that me, Malachai Parker, turned into one was that when I was born along with my twin in our very powerful witch family, I was born with the power to take magic from people instead of having my own. When my parents found out, I instantly got treated differently and grew up without affection or love. When I got older, I immediately turned into a sociopath with bad mentality. One day, my parents were out. I found out what they were hiding, so I killed my siblings apart from my loved twin.

Yasmina Rosu (11)
Great Yarmouth Charter Academy, Great Yarmouth

THE STORY BEHIND MALEFICENT

That big superhero act was all a huge lie. Sleeping Beauty was never as good as people thought. I'm the true superhero! Just think about it... All she did was find Merriweather in the house fire. I put out the fire, saved the fairies from a tornado, made medicines to fix every illness in the world and sent them to every country. The only things I did wrong were occasionally annoying people, curse Sleeping Beauty and put all of France to sleep for 100 years. So I moved away and had a child named after me: Maleficent!

Frejya McCluskey (11)
Great Yarmouth Charter Academy, Great Yarmouth

THE TRUE IDENTITY

That superhero act was all a lie. These stupid people really thought I was a good guy. I feel so bad for that so-called 'villain'. The only option was to frame him. I couldn't let my true self get caught.

Today, I will win. I will achieve my goal no matter what. I must not lose...

In the end, I did win. May have spilt some blood, but there was no other option. Watching him scream in pain was so satisfying. Seeing his eyes tear up as if they were in an ocean, flowing. My pain has now finally gone.

Angel Wilkin (12)
Great Yarmouth Charter Academy, Great Yarmouth

REFLECTION

I'm a schoolgirl, nothing much. When I brush my teeth before school, I stare into the mirror and see me. It's discomforting seeing the same me. I'm not sure, I might be crazy, but... is that really me? Do I really know who I am? Am I my true self? My fake self? Am I really the cheerful, chatty girl I think I am? Or am I disgraceful? Are there two sides of me? Sometimes I feel like destroying everything in my way, but sometimes I'm like stuck between a glass wall. Is this the true evil reality?

Gerda Skiragyte (11)
Great Yarmouth Charter Academy, Great Yarmouth

BRITE'S RETURN TO BUSINESS

One night in prison, I had a nightmare. I couldn't cut it out. There was a red wall. I pushed it, it disappeared and I woke up.

I went to the hall for breakfast. I ate it whole. It wasn't me. There was a force controlling me. As I was walking around, I saw an offender getting attacked. Before I knew it, I was dragging a person away. My powers were back.

That night, I walked to the gate. I opened it and ran. The Department of Security had failed. I was back and ready to get my revenge...

Thomas Malins (14)

Great Yarmouth Charter Academy, Great Yarmouth

LIFE'S EPIPHANY

Death takes people away. No matter how they perish, he guides them to their eternity. I put them on Earth, I give them life, emotion and love. I decide who they become and how they act. But I also choose how they die. I decide their pain. I am the reason people they love die, why children cry, why wars begin. It is only now that I realise that I am the cause of death itself. If I had never given essence to humans, no pain would be in this world. Death relieves humans of pain I inflict upon them.

Alyssa Basset-Oldfield (13)
Great Yarmouth Charter Academy, Great Yarmouth

VICTIM TO VILLAIN

My friend, Alora, never really belonged. She was always bullying others, but I knew why. She only did it to fit in. School life was hard for her. All of the cool kids would pick on her if she did not do acts like bullying. The cool kids are the villain really. She tried so hard to be able to not have to become a bully (like tried homeschooling), but she did so to survive. She was so innocent, but she is now evil. She came from the victim of bullying to the villain who does the bullying.

Chloe Ashworth (15)
Great Yarmouth Charter Academy, Great Yarmouth

JUSTICE

Well... well... well... From a distance, it looks like happily ever after does exist after all... despite what I have previously been told.
That's until I avenge my father for everything they did to him. They think keeping him locked away will keep evil away, but just you wait. I'm the weapon they don't even know exists... yet. Our so-called heroes haven't seen anything yet.

Rhys Saiche (16)
Great Yarmouth Charter Academy, Great Yarmouth

PIECES

I was in my lair. I did it to survive... *Boom!* The door fell down in pieces, splintering around the room. My sister strode in, twin to be exact, also known as... my nemesis. "Miss me?" she boomed.

"Miss you?" I replied. "I think you got yourself a fan club there," I said. She looked back and saw thousands of people staring. "Never mind."

"You need to kill your child..."

Silence... I screamed, "*No! Why would I?*"

"You'll die," she replied. In the other room, Alex cried, startled. "Why do I need to murder my own baby?" I gasped. Silence...

Megan Harvey (13)
St Ives School, Higher Tregenna

THE MURDEROUS LIE

"That superhero act was all a lie," he said. "You lie, cheat and twist the truth to fit your deranged reality." Anger filled his voice. Tears filled his eyes. "You live in a dream but don't realise how it hurts us, you're a psychopathic murderer who puts peoples' lives in danger!"
"You're wrong. I'm the hero," she denied.
"Fine, you want a villain?" he scoffed. "I'll be your villain." He lunged at her with his dagger but hit the wall of the castle. He lunged again. He didn't miss. Their eyes met as his arm retracted. The psychotic nightmare ended.

Evie Oatham (14)

St Ives School, Higher Tregenna

NURSERY RHYMES

I watched as she entered the room. My plan was in motion. I spoke to her over the speaker: "You are now trapped here until you complete three twisted challenges based on nursery rhymes." The doors opened into the first room. 'Baa Baa Black Sheep'. "You must kill sheep and deliver their wool." She completed it in a flash, though covered in blood. Next is 'This Little Piggy'. "Chase the piggy home and kill him." This took longer. I was pleased. She screamed, "*You are sick!*" Ha, foolish child.

Humpty-dumpty. No context. She fell off the wall and died. *Victory!*

Gwen Fryer (11)

St Ives School, Higher Tregenna

ACERBIC AI

They covered their ears. Rock music blasted out of Alexa's speakers, with three unblocked swears a second. "Alexa, stop!" they shouted. Nothing happened. They could see the despicable machine grinning, although there were 2mm-layers of plastic between them. The adults threw insults, adding to the noise, as innocent children laughed. It took several attempts to stop her from playing the disgusting music, and at this time the children were on the floor, crying, and their parents were literally begging on the floor for her mercy.

It seemed that she finally saw reason, and stopped on her horrible, terrible rampage.

Leo Kirk-Mackrell (12)
St Ives School, Higher Tregenna

HOW? I WONDER

A twig snapped under my feet. He turned around, I arose, aiming my rifle at his heart. "You killed my son, my wife, and broke my heart, now you pay."

"Please..." He stumbled back.

"Don't move!" I shouted, birds fleeing fearfully from my ferocity. The sun gleamed through the pine, a gentle breeze lulling as calm birdsong filled the region.

"It's too late," he stated, tears rolling down his cheeks. He fell. His body floating down the river, it would eventually go into Poseidon's possession.

To this day, I wonder if he jumped, or if it was merely a stumble.

Rowan Kemp (12)
St Ives School, Higher Tregenna

MALEFICENT'S JOURNAL

I, Maleficent, sat in this lonely dump of a cave until the fire fairies came bursting into the pitch-black cave. They said, "*Oi, you*, come here. You are going to jail for kidnapping children and killing them."

"*What?* I would never do that to innocent children! *Jail?* No, I am not going and you can't make me."

"Yes, we can, you horrible person! You have to come whether you like it or not."

"Okay, I will come to jail. I will only on one condition. I get to get out after one day."

"Unfortunately you cannot..."

Freya-Lilly Powell (12)
St Ives School, Higher Tregenna

SPIDERS ARE VICIOUS...

One... more... hit... Iron Man was down on the ground, coughing up blood. I punched him, my fist cracking and breaking. I heard his jaw crack... or my hand. I couldn't tell, I just kept going. Mushing him into the ground. *"No more Iron Man!"* I yelled. With my last breath of energy, I crushed his head, blood everywhere, brains like scrambled eggs, unearthly fluids seeping through the cracks of my fingers. No more heroes, no more justice, no more Avengers. I looked up, showered in blood. A sparkly circle. Through it, a caped figured silhouette in light.

"Hello... Peter."

Solomon Richards (12)
St Ives School, Higher Tregenna

SCARY STORY

Bang! I'd busted in. "Brother, I'm coming!" I shouted. "Who are you?" A shout came from upstairs in the two-storey house. I thumped up the stairs, I was going to kill him for what he did. I had a look to find nothing. He had gone. I whipped my wand out and glared into the jammed lock. I pointed my wand at the wood-carved door. *Boom!* The door flew off its hinges, crashing into my brother. "Ouch! That hurt, you psycho!" I'd terminated the door and watched the quivering hands raise.
"I'm going to kill you. *Kill!*"

Alfie Smith (11)
St Ives School, Higher Tregenna

I WON

"I've won and there's nothing you can do about it," I said.
"I'm not so sure," said Matt. Normally, that would have thrown me off, leading to my failure.
That may have happened. "Don't be smart with me, boy," I said in my most malicious voice.
"I'm not, I'm just stating the truth," replied Matt with a smirk on his face. I'd had enough. I started to use my magic on him. Even though he has natural immunity, he would still be feeling pain. Then he threw something at me, and my world went black. I had lost! Oh no...

Yves Armstrong-Donaldson (12)
St Ives School, Higher Tregenna

THE CROWN

As I travelled across the isolated marshes, the icy rain mercilessly slashed onto the dark forests of this moonlit night. My mind wandered. Was I doing the right thing? I turned a corner and there it stood, the immense stone walls, the giant towers; the castle! I cautiously entered through the wooden entrance into the abandoned parlour. The crooked floorboards eerily creaked and the wind howled as though it was laughing at me. I searched the room, feeling panicked, then a sudden shimmer caught my eye! I couldn't believe it. I stared, feeling hypnotised by its glow; the crown...

Gracie Dorrell (13)
St Ives School, Higher Tregenna

YOU WOULDN'T KNOW

She strutted along the street, heels clacking on the pavement, hair blowing gently in the breeze. In the darkness of the late hour, street lamps flickered. You wouldn't know who she was. You wouldn't know her plot. You wouldn't know what she was walking away from. She smirked, remembering what she had just done. She giggled. It was a sweet giggle. An innocent one. You wouldn't know what she was planning. Turning the corner and lightly floating up the steps, she was there. She was home. You wouldn't know she had just paid the assassin. The villain hides it well.

Maggie Mansell (12)
St Ives School, Higher Tregenna

THE MURDERER

I never really belonged in a mental asylum.
As soon as I had the knife, I killed everyone. Blood
everywhere, I escaped and saw a house. I watched them
and I attacked; so easy and so fun. Next house, same thing:
stalk, kill. My knife bloody and my hands dirty, I walked
down the street and saw a boy. "Hello," he said.
"Hello, child. Follow me, I have sweets."
"Okay!" I lured him to the asylum and showed him where I
lived. "What is this place?" he asked.
"The place where you will meet a gory, bloody, sad death..."

Tyler Barrett (12)
St Ives School, Higher Tregenna

OLD MAN ARTHUR

The old man opened the door and was surprised by a fast flood knocking him over, causing severe pain. Being drenched by the ceaseless water clogging his throat, he coughed and coughed until all of the water came out, allowing him to breathe once again. That's what he thought, although unexpectedly a big, big, big rush of water poured out of his neck. His brother entered the room and was extremely shocked at what happened to his good old brother Arthur.

Once the fast floods finished, relentless rain poured. After the brothers left hospital, they lived happily ever after.

Harvey Williams (13)
St Ives School, Higher Tregenna

WHAT HAVE I DONE?

I turned the corner into the damp parlour, cold, stiff. A man stood on the rug, cast into shadow. I remember her face, her fear, her screams.

"Why did you do it?" came his voice from the shadows.

"I did it to survive." But I didn't believe myself. I knew it wasn't true. A single candle dimly lit the room. He chuckled, eerie and merciless. Chills crawled over my body. Boots thumped against the floorboards as he crept closer, sensing my fear. I could feel warm breathing. A hand touched my face. For once, I don't know what might happen...

Fearne Slade (14)

St Ives School, Higher Tregenna

FRAMED

He appeared, a human, towering over me like the Burj Khalifa. I knew my fate was inevitable. There was nothing to do. I'm done for.

"Argh!" he screamed, running off, then an even bigger human came running with what looked like a giant stick with sharp bristles on the end. He chased me around the house infinitely until he got me, one of the bristles went through my leg. "That's what you deserve!" he said. I was devastated. The people who I look up to are actually evil. Wow, I can't believe it. This beautiful planet is actually quite scary.

Kai Austin (12)
St Ives School, Higher Tregenna

THE TWISTED TRUTH OF RED RIDING HOOD

She was screaming. Screaming in pain as I swallowed her whole silence.

I awoke with a jolt, groaning. Another dream. I wouldn't ever forget who I was. I was the monster. The villain everyone had nightmares about. But I didn't want to be. Starting over was impossible. Getting up and padding over to the entrance of my den, crisp autumn leaves crunched underfoot. Stopping suddenly, I noticed a girl walking towards me. She was alone. Looking closer, I saw red fabric by her side. A cape. My heart stopped as I saw her hand gripped around something shiny and sharp...

Chloe Wills (12)
St Ives School, Higher Tregenna

I JUST WANT TO ESCAPE

I just want to escape; I didn't mean to hurt them. Callous mist rolled across the isolated forest, surrounding my mansion. Adventurous, the group crept through the decrepit window. I saw their torches shining down the long hallways. I knew it was my time. Selfishly, I knocked over a stack of boxes. A cacophony of screams flooded the mansion. I headed towards the grand staircase where the chandelier hung. I nudged it, it swung. The group ascended upstairs. I collided with the chandelier and it fell. It crushed them. I just want to escape; I didn't mean to hurt them.

Danielle Fox (14)
St Ives School, Higher Tregenna

URSULA'S STORY

I never really belonged to pure evil; my sweet, beautiful, innocent little self singing softly in my small, cramped room. Loyal friends, amazing house with vibrant colours in every direction until an outstanding little baby with bold, dark red locks of hair. Everyone paid attention to her... Ariel. As the years went past, I was a forgotten outcast who lived in a dark underwater cave miles away from the people singing, dancing, laughter all without me... that evil child. She stole everything from me; my loyal friends, my family, my life. She is why I went pure rotten evil.

Katie Cook (12)
St Ives School, Higher Tregenna

BEGINNING

In the beginning, there was me. I've watched over humans forever, but I've never seen anything like Alex. This is his story.

As he walked down the corridor, he noticed the trap holes in the wall. Probably nets. He rolled a stone, the trap activated. As he walked, he set the bomb. One minute to get out. He ran to the doorway and ducked, there was a red button. That was why he was here. He pressed it, men ran to him.

"What have you done? You have unleashed the Plague, an infection." *Boom!* "You have brought the death day..."

Etienne Fulker (11)
St Ives School, Higher Tregenna

THE DEVIL'S LIGHT

That superhero act was all a lie. She betrayed her own sister and no one ever forgot it... Samera (the wicked witch of the west) was an extremely intimidating, horrid and evil woman. Well, as some would say, a 'monster'. She was hated by so many people after what she had done.

Let me explain. One day, a beautiful woman (named Hally) arrived at the place, Harvard. Samera wasn't happy about this and made a promise to her sister. A promise that she obviously couldn't keep. That same day, Hally was found dead in her room. Something bad had happened...

Phoebe Bradbury (12)
St Ives School, Higher Tregenna

BATMAN MEETS 'OLD LADY'

It was a rainy, depressing evening in a small, creepy, castaway bungalow. As the rain slowly came to a halt, a strange presence appeared. There was Batman! Eventually, the presence ceased as Batman reached for the door handle of the derelict building. As he reached out, he was startled by the movement of shadows inside the building. He stood back as the door unsealed. There was a small old lady standing in the doorway. She lunged at Batman, holding a knife coated with blood. Batman grabbed the old lady's wrist and stole the knife. "Who are you?" he said.

Rupert Bell (13)
St Ives School, Higher Tregenna

EXPLOSION

I wasn't proud of what I'd done, but I couldn't let these girls find out. There are four of them. There were five, but that's my problem.

I put together the things I needed to scare them the next day. I waited until dark before posting my twisted gifts through their letterboxes. After house four, it started lashing down hailstones. They dug into my skin like knives as I cycled unsteadily home. I thought it would be easy keeping it a secret; it wasn't. I told them the next day. I said, "I'm sorry I made your best friend explode!"

Olive A-Chapman (13)
St Ives School, Higher Tregenna

ACE OF SPADES

Okay, let's just get one thing straight; I didn't actually intend on killing my best friend - I just saw the opportunity and took it. God only knows how I haven't been caught; it was a sloppy job, like really sloppy - overly sloppy. And because of my actions, I'm wishing I had been caught - I *need* to be punished for what I did, what I shouldn't have done. It felt horrible, but that feeling of power - it was amazing! Knowing you held the cards for someone else's life. But it was *her* life and I had to take it - a necessity!

Ysella Thomas (12)
St Ives School, Higher Tregenna

THE UNFORTUNATE GARDENER

Once, there were two gardeners whose gardens were the neatest, most glamorous you have ever seen. Each year, both men would enter the local garden competition and each year they would share first prize. But one year, that changed. One of the men became greedy and ambitious. Wanting to win for himself, he crept into his neighbour's garden and chopped down his prize oak tree. The humongous tree, with so much weight, tumbled to the ground and crushed the selfish gardener and his chainsaw flat. This left the good gardener free to win the competition every year.

Laurence Wallis (12)
St Ives School, Higher Tregenna

RACE

I was in the lead, the final race of the British championship. I was about to win the British championship, my dream, my future of the moment, until disaster struck. There were five laps to go and I could hear this weird high-pitched buzz from behind me. The noise had been there for a couple of laps now, but when I looked back, nothing was there. I thought it could have possibly been my engine moving forward and the chain slackening off. It wasn't that though. *Bang!* Something hit my rear. It flipped my kart. My race over, future damaged...

Martin Wright (12)
St Ives School, Higher Tregenna

MEDUSA'S DAY OFF

Before I became this snake-haired diabolical creature who turned people to stone, I was a regular girl with a regular dream. It's ironic really. I wanted to be a hairdresser. Today's my day off. I'm going to throw my sunglasses on (preventing any people-turning-to-stone issues) and head down to my local salon for my monthly trim and snakeskin highlights. Once the clients get over their fear of having Medusa at the next washbasin, I can relax and just be me. I always leave tips; it can't be easy having to put up with me obviously!

Edie Price (12)
St Ives School, Higher Tregenna

THE RAT MAN

Sirens sounded, cars sped past to the NYC university and there I was, running out of the university, chemicals in hand, looking like a rat. And you wonder how I got here? Well, let's go back to the beginning. It all started one day when I was working late at the lab, working on my project Rat - rat enhancing technology, when suddenly the experiment went wrong and an explosion happened.

I woke up ten days later in the ER, I had suffered major injuries. Later that day, I felt sick and suddenly I started transforming. I rushed home and saw...

Will Bramwell (13)
St Ives School, Higher Tregenna

THE CALL FOR HELP

I can't believe it. I never would have thought it. It couldn't be, could it? H-how did they do that? They commanded the unbeatable stone army. The stone army was of legend, an old one. When Ying and Yang were still one, the stone army was destroying the Ying and Yang, making the balance shift. So Ying and Yang divided and locked the power to control them in one island and the army in the other. But someone unlocked *both areas!* They control the whole world now. Their name is Ash Jackson! I have to go now! Send help! *Beep...*

Freya Scorer (13)
St Ives School, Higher Tregenna

THE ORIGIN OF PINEAPPLE THE EVIL CAT

It began at a school with a cat named Pineapple that had been bullied. He had been picked on by humans who tugged on his tuft of hair that resembled a pineapple. When his craving for revenge (and pineapples) developed, he created the catsuit to rid the world of humans. Meanwhile, his neighbour, Doge had developed doggy powers and he noticed Pineapple turning evil. As Doge went to check on his friend, he heard the suit whirring so he burst through the door. A fire broke out. Pineapple didn't want to hurt his friend, so he teleported far away...

Toby Wilkinson (12)
St Ives School, Higher Tregenna

DO YOU LOVE ME NOW?

I never looked the same as everyone else. Shocked eyes followed me everywhere I walked. I was created differently with caution. Only she treated me normally, but I had pushed her away. I was an outcast purely because I wasn't porcelain and white like them. I would prove my devotion to her.

The next day, I congregated with my so-called peers. I reached into my bag and pulled it out. I held the trigger down. There was no one left but me and her. "Do you love me now? At last, it's just us! Finally, we'll be free together!"

Ashley Davies (14)
St Ives School, Higher Tregenna

142

CAUGHT IN A TWISTED ACT

This is twisted... How did it get to this? It was 8 in the morning, my sister, Anastasia, had gotten orders from our wicked mother to kill Cinderella before the royal ball began. Anastasia being too scared, I decided to do it myself. I stormed into the kitchen, pulling out a knife from one of the thousands of wooden drawers. I stepped quickly up the stone stairs. I tightened my grip on the sharp blade. Cinderella's metal door creaked open to reveal a sat girl. I lifted the knife higher. Cinderella turned, horrified. How did it get to this?

Brooke Bonner (12)
St Ives School, Higher Tregenna

I HAD TO GET HER BACK

I still haven't forgotten when my coach Jess told me that I would never be good enough to progress onto the next group. That made me determined. So I moved clubs and made it my mission to prove her wrong. I made my legs straighter, extended my toes and fingers, and jumped higher.

Competition day arrived and Jess was there. That's when the nerves kicked in. She looked at me, I looked at her. That was all the motivation I needed. The competition began, and I had four clean rounds. I looked her in the eyes, standing in first place.

Kiki Fox (11)
St Ives School, Higher Tregenna

DEMON BRINGER

It was a difficult day. I had to get across the lava dunes to summon monsters by the ruin. I rest as I hear my demons terrorising my town. I realise. My brother. I forgot to open the bunker for him! He's unsafe. I run out. I hear his screams. I run as quickly as I can. I see him, he screams, "*Big brother, help!*" Before I could say anything, my monster says, "Master," and bows to me. My brother saw. He would tell everyone, so I knew I had to kill him.
"I'm sorry, brother. Please forgive me."

Andy Sully (12)
St Ives School, Higher Tregenna

CALLAHAN'S PLAN

My plan was in motion. I was finally going to get my daughter back. After years, she had been stuck in a mysterious world. I got to use amazing inventions thanks to the students in the technology department and the science department. Hopefully all thanks to them I will get my daughter back. She's all I have left... Since she left, I have exercised my mind to a calmer state. After all this, we shall go on a nice long walk. *I hope those pesky teenagers don't disturb this*, I thought as I pressed on the button of the machine...

Lily Ferris (13)
St Ives School, Higher Tregenna

OLD MAN ARTHUR

The old man opened the door and was surprised with a fast flood knocking him over, causing him severe pain. Old man Arthur was drenched by the ceaseless water clogging his throat. He coughed and coughed until all of the water came out. Although that's what he thought, unexpectedly a big, big, big rush of water poured out of his neck! His brother entered the room and was extremely shocked at what had happened to his good old brother Arthur. Then another wave came and took out the brother with a wild wave. This sent them to the hospital.

Mason Aldrich (13)
St Ives School, Higher Tregenna

FAIREST OF THEM ALL

I strutted down the aisle, embracing gasps from the awe-struck crowd. It was my wedding day. Feeling like a queen, I glided down the marble steps, gazing at the handsome man soon to be my husband. As my fingers lifted the shimmering veil away from my face, he froze. "I shan't marry her! I was promised the fairest of them all!" He glanced with a look of pure hatred before leaving me at the altar, tears welling in my eyes. He made everything clear. I must become the fairest of them all. I felt like a queen. An evil queen...

Lucie Cole (12)
St Ives School, Higher Tregenna

LIE

The superhero act was all a lie. My plan is coming together perfectly. It all started when I was left by my friends. Everyone forgot about me and I was left in the shadows. One day, I had a think and I couldn't live like this anymore. I started small by generally keeping people safe. But now I'm known for being the best 'god' superhero alive. Although little does anyone know this is all an act. People will remember me and I will rise in power! I'm so close to being the most powerful person in the whole entire world.

Maddison Franklin (12)
St Ives School, Higher Tregenna

THE ISLAND

It had been a week or two after the portal had opened. This island was weird and on another level. The cave was by far the strangest, and that was where I got transformed. The walls were filled with multicoloured gems, but what scared me were the ghosts. At first I thought I was hallucinating, but no. The literal ghosts of Bin Laden, Hitler and Stalin came swooping out of nowhere and I just felt a weird feeling... I felt empowered. They were inside my soul.
I crept out and that night the air was pierced with short-cut screams...

Elliot Symons (13)

St Ives School, Higher Tregenna

WILL I EVER BELONG?

I never really belonged anywhere. People would always laugh at me. Even the family I was born into. One day, I was tripped up over a bridge. It was then, when I entered the water, that I discovered a person like me. Misunderstood, laughed at. They taught me to stand up for myself.
I walked along the street, people began to mock me once again. I had had enough! I walked over to some corrupt people and stabbed them in the chest. Everyone stared at me. I laughed. I had become the villain. What an absolutely wonderful way to live.

Isla Thornton (12)
St Ives School, Higher Tregenna

THE HULK

As Hulk was testing his strength on a testing dummy, his lights went out and came back on. He didn't know what happened, so he carried on. Minutes later, he got bit on the elbow by a leathery black bat. He pushed the bat off but it was too quick. Suddenly, Dracula appeared and bit his hand! The Hulk punched Dracula, it didn't affect him. He carried on and bit the Hulk on the leg, making him fall over. 5:59am... The Hulk escaped, finding some prep lime to repair himself. The sun rose and Dracula began to melt. Hulk won.

Caleb Woodcroft (13)
St Ives School, Higher Tregenna

IN THE WOODS

Subjected to years of abuse from his demonic parents, Hansel wanted his own life back. He was fed up with wearing rags for clothing, scarce food and getting locked up. The invisible rage inside him caused him to go on killing sprees with a kitchen knife at rabbits and other wildlife. It reached a tipping point when his parents were arguing and they decided to leave him in a forest. When he ventured his way back, he stumbled across an old rusty axe. Using the last of his strength to lift the axe, as his mum rushed out, he struck...

Isaac Walsh (12)
St Ives School, Higher Tregenna

THE TRUTH IS INSIDE

It was pitch-black, the trees were whistling in my ear as I regretfully crept up to the eerie and broken-down castle. I still haven't forgotten when my friend had been brutally murdered. I had to go back in and do what was right. I then opened the creaky door and entered. I saw a black figure run across the hallway. I knew I wasn't alone. The sinister corridors and smashed windows made me tremble in fear. I got to the dark room and then remembered this was the creepy room my friend died in. Then I saw *them*...

Ethan Quinn (14)
St Ives School, Higher Tregenna

WICKED

I still remember. I ran to the back of my car and flung open the trunk to see him still tied up, struggling to break free. A ball shoved so far into his mouth it broke his jaw. I laughed hysterically, unable to stop. I've never laughed this hard in my life. My dry lips split open as I screamed out happiness. Blood had gone all over his face. "Who's the weak one now?" I screamed. My eyes widened. "This is my perfect victory." I yanked him out and smirked at him as I carried him away by his legs...

Rocky Palmer (12)
St Ives School, Higher Tregenna

THE QUEEN'S BROKEN HEART

I never really belonged... Every day since I was two and Mirana came along, she was always the favourite and I was looked down on. Once, when I was crying, Mother told me, "Elizabeth, you should never cry. Crying is for babies and you're not a baby, are you? Or, well, I don't think so." Now I am older and it is still the same, but Mother and Father are dead now. The real reason they died is that they were poisoned by Mirana in their sleep, and I took the blame! Now I'm neglected and alone in my castle.

Camilla Bennie Louise (12)

St Ives School, Higher Tregenna

GHOST!

There was once a small girl named Penelope. She lived with her small family in a small town, down Ghost Street! Now, the plot twist is that Penelope and everyone who lives on Ghost Street are ghosts. Every Halloween, the people of the town go out and instead of trick-or-treating, they haunt people. But *not* in a bad way. Instead of creeping people out, they try to make friends with the humans, but every human they touch becomes a ghost. Sadly, the people of Ghost Street do not know this and they keep on haunting.

Willow Tarplee (12)
St Ives School, Higher Tregenna

I WAS ALONE, OR SO I THOUGHT...

It was midnight. I was on my way to Waitrose, walking along the side of the road where cars sped at supernatural speeds. I stopped. I shuddered. There was a figure looming in the darkness. It was striding towards me when I realised it was holding a gun. Finger poised on the trigger, I had no other choice but to back out into the road. Still the figure remained, to corner me. There was nowhere to run. I was right in the centre of the road now; desolate, remote, rarely used. Suddenly, a black truck came at us full speed...

Dylan Kemp (13)
St Ives School, Higher Tregenna

THE JOKER...

I'm having a day off from killing... Why do people care about life so much? Every day the same old thing, do they not get bored? My life's amazing; I can do anything I want. I am going to go for a walk... Hopefully I don't bump into the police like every time I go outside... Wow, I never thought I could do that - I just robbed a bank without killing someone. Ugh, here come the police... What is it with them these days?

Well, I guess I broke that promise. One person dead, another one dead. How many more?

Teddy Nichols (13)
St Ives School, Higher Tregenna

AM I THE ONE?

One night, I was left home alone and I heard banging in the distance and I wondered what it was, so I put my coat on and left and crept slowly towards where it was coming from. The moonlight seemed different to usual. Very different. I looked at my hands the moonlight was changing me. Everyone started coming out of their houses, running down to the sea. They're all werewolves! I looked at my hands again, I had claws and furry hands. I was turning into a werewolf too! Everyone stopped and stared at me. Am I the one?

Harriet Hartley (12)
St Ives School, Higher Tregenna

MENTAL STATE

A one-time opportunity turned into a life sentence times seven. But no one can keep me in here. Not unless I'm stupid. Now, the cell. The cell has a corner full of cobwebs, a toilet without a flush, and the last thing in the room: the bed. The dull, unwanted bed. Although my bed is awful, the security is worse.
I managed to stab an inmate to death. I believe that was fair game. A new therapist came. My condition is worse, my mental state is bad. He told me my screw are loose and that I should *die*...

Archie Cooper (12)
St Ives School, Higher Tregenna

THE DARK WOODS

I still haven't forgotten the day I ventured into the woods with my friend and made it out alone. It was a normal day when my friend wanted to explore the woods. Before they disappeared, I remember seeing a human-like body but hairy and muscly like a werewolf. I could not tell. I heard screaming and like a sort of breeze or something breathing on me! I started running, running far away. I made it out alone. There have been investigations every day but there has never been any evidence. I live in fear to this day.

Ophelia Musto Shinton (11)
St Ives School, Higher Tregenna

THE BASEMENT

Silence. Nothing but silence. All of those screams soon turned into moans. But now silence. The smoke from the fire half filled the room until it reached the air pocket above. Sat in my chair, hands on my lap. Thinking, one mistake led to many. I made my choices and now it is too late. Now there is no turning back. Those people, the ones I used, still lay there in the basement. No one there to find them. They played their part. Now it's time to play mine, you see. The thing is, it all began in the basement...

Gabriel Musto-Shinton (13)

St Ives School, Higher Tregenna

EVIL

What is this place? Where am I? Well, I'm lying in a bed, dressed in a white gown. Next to the bed I see two things: a clipboard and a scalpel. I place the scalpel in my pocket and read the clipboard. It says something about a psychopath and a coma... *Scream*. A child? I walk to the other room, a baby in a small crib alone. I feel a horrible urge... to kill. Scalpel... I grip the knife... *Stab!* I'm a murderer. Filled with self-pity, I weep for myself. Just one-
Stab! Black.

Will Clayton (12)
St Ives School, Higher Tregenna

THE SCARY HUNTER!

It's so cold. I don't like Christmas. Gunshots echoed through the trees as crows scarpered from the branches. I turned and saw a scary man, he looked insane with scratches on his face. I jumped into a bush as he walked past through the trees. That's when I stepped on a stick. It made a noise, he found me. He held me down, pointing his pistol at my heart. I kicked him back, snatched his gun, shooting him. I was scared but full of relief. He got up again, but I jumped out of a tree, kicking his head...

Rune Gustafsson (11)
St Ives School, Higher Tregenna

THE DEADLY TOUCH

I still haven't forgotten the day I went into the deathly forest full of the darkest shadows you would ever see. Out of these shadows appeared a boy. A tiny sad boy who was all alone. I instantly wanted to make him happy. I offered him my hand and he slowly moved his towards mine. As soon as I touched his icy cold hand, I suddenly felt a burning in my soul. Then he vanished. I dropped to the floor, I was alone. I wasn't myself anymore, I was sad and cold.
I sit waiting for someone else to appear...

Poppy Taylor (12)
St Ives School, Higher Tregenna

THE LOST CAT

Once upon a time, there lived a cat. The cat's name was Jeffery. Jeffery was black and white and had green eyes. His claws were as sharp as knives. Jeffery lives in the city with a kitten called Pig. Pig was young and mischievous. Every night, Jeffery would try and get rid of Pig as he was jealous of the attention Pig got.

One day, Pig got mad at Jeffery, so Pig stormed off with his thoughts. This was because Jeffery found a super soaker and pulled the trigger so Pig got wet.

But all is fine now!

Amiee Simpson (11)

St Ives School, Higher Tregenna

BULLETPROOF

Bang! Flames erupted from the car as it suddenly met its end. The sound of sirens blasted through my sweaty ears. What have I done? Why is this happening? What should I do? With the exhaust on the car pounding, I took one bloody hand off the wheel and reached for my gun. Two of the front tyres on the police car got hit. My trembling foot stepping on the accelerator, the engine of my car roared and I sped off into the horizon. If only I knew what awaited me. Two huge bulletproof police cars. Oh no...

Ollie Herbert (11)
St Ives School, Higher Tregenna

THE THREE LITTLE PIGS (OR AT LEAST WHAT'S LEFT OF THEM)

I never really belonged. I was always different ever since those wretched three little pigs. I destroyed their houses and now I have them right in my claws, ready for me to eat. Which one first? I walk over to my knife collection. Ah, this will do nicely. I pick up the biggest one I can find. How do I choose which piggy goes first? Eenie, meenie, miny, moe, catch a piggy by its toe. If it bites, slit its throat, eenie, meenie, miny, mo. I choose you. Well, this will be fun. Let's see what I can do...

Eachan Wilson (12)
St Ives School, Higher Tregenna

WHEN I BECAME THE VILLAIN

I still haven't forgotten. Forgotten the day I went from a loved hero to a despised outcast. A villain. I did it to survive. It was a gale; clouds covering the sky, rain drenching me in misery. I did it to survive, so others could survive. The hero was going to be the villain, I was going to be the hero. So I pushed him. I pushed him off the cliff into the dancing gale. I pushed him into the black-blue sea that swallowed him whole. Only I knew what he was. That was the night a villain was made.

Catrin Berriman (12)
St Ives School, Higher Tregenna

THE DOLL

We arrived at the camp. We broke into groups. One set up camp, the other searched the desolate abandoned town. Whilst the others set up the tents, me and my friends found an old toyshop full of old teddies. There was one doll in the centre of the room. This doll gave us a death stare. It sat with an evil smirk on its face that sent a fearful shiver down my spine. We entered the shop to see thousands of plastic eyes lasering down on us, then this creepy little doll started to move towards us...

Perran Metcalfe-Waller (13)

St Ives School, Higher Tregenna

THE BACKGROUND

At the age of eighteen, I got kicked out of my family house. I had to live with my friend who lent me a room and a computer for a while. This is when I changed... I found a small company that was buying people's personal data for ten dollars. I would stay up all night hacking and trying to earn money. I always felt bad for doing this, but I had to turn my life around and make some money. I have never felt appreciated or loved by anyone in my life. This wasn't my fault, I was forced...

Oscar Wills (12)
St Ives School, Higher Tregenna

172

POPO

As I sit in the dark alleyway, stalking my prey, my thirst for blood rages on. I slowly approach and get ready to kill. Someone sees me, so I chase them down and shank them with my nan's crusty butcher knife. They scream in pain, blood gushing from their wound. They're shaken in horror and hear the popo come after me. I see something with a swaggy iPhone 6 and I stare him down. He gets scared and runs to the nearest shop. I chase into the popo and I get shot. Rest in peace.

N J Nicholls (12)
St Ives School, Higher Tregenna

THE MONSTER IN A HOUSE

I was alone. I thought I got away, then I heard the monster's footsteps. He was after me. I had to get away. I ran upstairs to my broom and flew away, but the monster flew after me. Just then, I heard a car...? It was Ron. He drove into the monster and killed it, but we still had to save Harry. We got our mates and drove over. We had to get him and us to Hogwarts. We got to his house and beat back the bars on his window. He hopped in the car and we left.

Jack Thomas (12)
St Ives School, Higher Tregenna

THE KILLER

Every word said in my head told me to slice that knife in her heart. I am not a bad man, but the urge is killing me, my urge to kill. The blood dripping down from a cut-off limb after the death of this spoilt girl would please me more than anything else. Am I a bad person? I am starting to think that the people in the mental hospital were right. I am a bad person.

Long story short, she is dead.

Senara Beeson (13)
St Ives School, Higher Tregenna

ESCAPE!

The children? Where are they? I need them in my soup! Here they are.

"Hello children, I see you have seen my biscuit house."

"Yes, we love it!" shout the children. They don't know they are going to go in my soup being prepared in the room next door. "Come down into the kitchen."

"Wow! Grandma, that smells nice. What is it?" they question.

"Would you like soup?"

"Yeah..." Hansel and Gretel didn't sound convinced.

"You're going in there!" I shout, lifting Hansel up.

"*Nooo!*" He gets out. "You nasty snake! don't leave!" I scream and they leave like snakes.

Archie Morton (13)
Walton High Brooklands Campus, Brooklands

LITTLE RED RIDING HOOD

Once upon a time, there were three little pigs who were obsessed with blowing objects down, like people's houses, to entertain themselves. But what they didn't know was that they worsened day by day and that people were getting angry and frustrated. They wanted revenge but they didn't know how. The naughty pigs were huffing and puffing.
A year passed and no one had done anything. This was traumatizing for other citizens. One day, a pack of wolves came to the pigs' town. They were hungry! The pigs tried blowing them away, but it didn't work!
"You look delicious...!"

Zebbi Dixon-Osei (14)
Walton High Brooklands Campus, Brooklands

BAD CINDERELLA

Even after I tell this story, people won't understand. That's the problem. Everyone is always on the beautiful princess' side. But that 'beautiful' princess turned my life upside down. 'Ugly'. 'Awful'. 'Disgusting'. These are words I am used to hearing. All I wanted was a peaceful life with the prince. Cinderella destroyed my future. And nobody cares.

The public believes what they want to and makes it into a fairy tale. But they don't know the truth. Every false accusation is a dagger to my heart. All because of my stepsister...

Sophia Patsavellas (14)
Walton High Brooklands Campus, Brooklands

THE WITCH OF OZ

"I want a heart!" shouted the Tinman.

"I want a brain!" exclaimed the scarecrow, as there was nothing in his silly head but straw.

"I want courage!" cried the cowardly lion. However, naive Dorothy just wanted to go home. She seemed quite happy to help them all though. She merrily skipped along the yellow brick road in *my* shoes! They're rightfully mine since she murdered my sister and she wrongfully stole them from the Wicked Witch of the West. I have to remind Tinman and Scarecrow that Dorothy already had a heart and brain...

Skye Welsh (14)

Walton High Brooklands Campus, Brooklands

CHILDREN OF THE FOREST

The metal teeth sank into the base of the child's home and it fell, memories crashing to the muddy ground. He swung from branch to branch, the homes of other poor unfortunate souls plummeting to the ground. The child of the forest swung to the giant tree in the middle of the forest and looked around at the rampaging metal-toothed monsters and giant falling trees.

And when all homes fell, the giant tree stood tall, too strong for the monsters below. The child sat on a branch, looked around, and wept as silent as the forest...

Luther Brown
Walton High Brooklands Campus, Brooklands

THE OTHER SIDE

There she was, nestled within the prince's arms. That should be me. But I don't want it to be me. I didn't love the prince and I never would. But my mother wanted me to love him, to be the one he loves. And why? Because of money. Never love. Cinderella is what they called her. She was my 'sister', but my mother tore us apart. I did love someone; the baker. His smile is the light to my dark. I loved him, not the prince, but my mother would never agree. Love is what I fear.

Disha Kharod (14)
Walton High Brooklands Campus, Brooklands

MOTHER GOTHEL

Seeking youth was my first intention. I used to be loved and was surrounded by crowds in my past, but with every wrinkle I got, the more distant people were. I watched as people who adored me disappeared. So I came to the conclusion all they used to see in me was my beauty. I heard stories of a healing flower that could make you young again. And I wanted it. I had been searching for this precious flower for years, only when I found it, it got taken from me. All I wanted was my youth back.

Aaliyah Salum (13)

Walton High Brooklands Campus, Brooklands

WOLF

My dad wasn't that big or bad. He was just a wolf and I loved him. Mother Gothel took me from him when I was just a few weeks old. She made him bring the princess to her. But when he got to the castle, he couldn't do it. She gave him another chance. She made him kill the two pigs. He got the first two, but number three shot him in the arm. She gave him one more chance. He had to kill Little Red Riding Hood. I never saw him again.

Calum Pickett (13)
Walton High Brooklands Campus, Brooklands

LOKI AND THOR

Loki just killed his brother Thor with a knife. Loki knew that everyone would hate him, but Loki knew that he had done the right thing. Thor was planning to kill Loki, but Loki realised just in time. If Loki did not kill Thor, then Thor would have killed Loki, his parents, and destroyed Asgard. Loki had always seemed rude, but this was because his parents favoured Thor in nearly every matter and because of that he was never nice or kind.

Shahmeer Khattak (13)
Walton High Brooklands Campus, Brooklands

YoungWriters
Est. 1991

YOUNG WRITERS
INFORMATION

We hope you have enjoyed reading this book – and
that you will continue to in the coming years.

If you're a young writer who enjoys reading and creative
writing, or the parent of an enthusiastic poet or story writer,
do visit our website **www.youngwriters.co.uk**. Here you
will find free competitions, workshops and games, as well
as recommended reads, a poetry glossary and our blog.
There's lots to keep budding writers motivated to write!

If you would like to order further copies of this book,
or any of our other titles, then please give us a
call or order via your online account.

Young Writers
Remus House
Coltsfoot Drive
Peterborough
PE2 9BF
(01733) 890066
info@youngwriters.co.uk

Join in the conversation!
Tips, news, giveaways and much more!

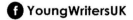 YoungWritersUK  YoungWritersCW  youngwriterscw